"Emm...

Emma didn't look happy to see Benjamin at all.

He frowned. "I'm sorry. I didn't startle you, did I? My goat got into the garden and I just..."

Her green eyes were wide and they did not have their usual sparkle. Her cheeks had lost their rosy color. And her skin seemed pale.

He backed away a step and lowered his voice. "Are you okay? I didn't mean to..." He wanted to reach out and take her hand. "I'm really sorry about that. I know I startled you. But, uh..." He looked away and scratched his jaw. "It's really *gut* to see you again." He looked back at her and saw her hand drift down to her belly.

His eyes followed her hand and he noticed a round bulge beneath her purple cape dress.

A baby bump.

Benjamin froze. He had no idea what to say. His eyes flicked back up to hers and he understood the expression on her face now.

Emma stared back for a moment, then shook her head, turned around...and fled.

After **Virginia Wise**'s oldest son left for college and her youngest son began high school, she finally had time to pursue her dream of writing novels. Virginia dusted off the keyboard she once used as a magazine editor and journalist to create a world that combines her love of romance, family and Plain living. Virginia loves to wander Lancaster County's Amish country to find inspiration for her next novel. While home in Northern Virginia, she enjoys painting, embroidery, taking long walks in the woods, and spending time with family, friends and her husband of almost twenty-five years.

Books by Virginia Wise

Love Inspired

An Amish Christmas Inheritance
The Secret Amish Admirer
Healed by the Amish Nanny
A Home for His Amish Children
The Amish Baby Scandal

Visit the Author Profile page at LoveInspired.com for more titles.

THE AMISH
BABY SCANDAL

VIRGINIA WISE

LOVE INSPIRED
INSPIRATIONAL ROMANCE

LOVE INSPIRED®
INSPIRATIONAL ROMANCE

Recycling programs
for this product may
not exist in your area.

ISBN-13: 978-1-335-93200-6

The Amish Baby Scandal

Love Inspired
22 Adelaide St. West, 41st Floor
Toronto, Ontario M5H 4E3, Canada
www.LoveInspired.com

Printed in U.S.A.

I will praise thee; for I am fearfully
and wonderfully made: marvellous are thy works;
and that my soul knoweth right well.
—*Psalm* 139:14

To my sons

Chapter One

Benjamin Stoltzfus pulled on one of his boots, lost his balance, and hopped in place to regain his footing. He leaned a shoulder against the kitchen door to pull on his second boot while he listened to the clang of pots and pans alongside the low murmur of his sisters' voices. His hand was on the doorknob when he distinctly heard the words "Emma Yoder." He wasn't eavesdropping, but he couldn't help but overhear when they were talking right in front of him.

"Moved into the bishop's place for good," Benjamin's sister Miriam added. Then she glanced over her shoulder, saw him watching, and clamped her mouth shut.

Benjamin's hand dropped from the doorknob. "Emma's moved to Bluebird Hills?"

Miriam, Naomi, Leah, and Amanda all exchanged glances, but said nothing. Miriam adjusted the blue work kerchief covering her brown hair, then turned all her attention to the pot of soup simmering on the stove. Of his four sisters,

Leah was the one Benjamin was closest to, so he figured he had the best chance of getting information out of her.

"Leah, what about Emma? What's going on?" His belly did a little flip-flop at the thought of Emma living on the neighboring farm. Her home had always been in Ohio but, throughout their childhood, she had spent summers next door, helping out her aunt and uncle. Those visits had stopped a few years ago. And now, it wasn't even summer. Fall was on its way. She shouldn't be in town at all.

Leah sprinkled a pinch of thyme in the soup pot and frowned. "*Ach*, nothing. It's just that she's moved here to stay."

A bolt of joy shot through Benjamin. His face lit up in a grin before he remembered to hide his reaction from his nosy sisters. He forced his face into a neutral expression, but he couldn't stop the pounding of his heart. It was too good to be true. His lips twitched as he tried not to smile.

Miriam's eyebrows shot up. "Don't get any ideas, Benji. It would never work out." The oldest and most sensible of his sisters, she already had fine lines around her eyes and mouth, even though she was barely thirty. It was probably because she had taken on too much responsibility after their parents passed away. They had been on their way to a mud sale on the other side of Lancaster County when their hired *Englisch* driver wrecked the car. Miriam had raised Benjamin since he was twelve years old, and now all five siblings worked together to run the family goat farm.

"What? *Nee*. We're just friends. We've only ever been friends." He shifted his weight from one foot to the other. "Why, uh, would you ever think otherwise? That's ridiculous."

"Uh-huh." Miriam did not look convinced.

An uncomfortable realization zipped through Benjamin. "Wait, she's not gotten married, has she? That's not what you meant, is it? I haven't heard anything." He tugged at the neckline of his shirt. Had the kitchen been this hot a few minutes ago? The thought of Emma married to someone else made him feel overheated, like he had caught a sudden fever. Of course, they'd never courted. He would never expect someone like Emma to be interested in him. She was beautiful, popular, and utterly out of his league. He had always been happy to just be her friend. They had a wonderful time together and he had enjoyed getting to know her as a person, with no strings attached and no pressure to impress her. So, he wasn't prepared for how tough it was to imagine her married to someone else.

His sisters didn't answer right away. Amanda wiped her hands on her apron, then stood on her tiptoes to whisper something in Naomi's ear. Amanda was small with dark features and she always moved quickly, like a bird, which made Benjamin seem even slower. Naomi was tall and thin, the opposite of Amanda, but her dark hair and eyes marked them as siblings. Benjamin watched them both with a frown on his face. Amanda straightened back up and cleared her throat. "Why don't you go on and feed the goats?"

"Why don't you tell me what's going on with Emma?" Benjamin shot back.

Amanda waved him away, and turned her attention to the stove. There was an uncomfortable silence.

"Well, is she married or not?" Benjamin asked.

"Nee," Leah said. "She isn't married." She picked up a yellow dish towel and began wiping the butcher-block counter.

"Oh, *gut.*" Benjamin realized his mistake as soon as he said the words. He knew better than to let his sisters know how he felt about a woman. If they didn't tease him mercilessly, they would meddle in the relationship—or lack of relationship, to be more accurate. "I mean, that's *gut* for her, I guess. I mean, I hadn't heard she was courting anyone." Benjamin took off his straw hat, ran his fingers through his dark brown hair, and pushed his hat back onto his head. He wasn't doing a very good job of backtracking.

"Not anyone Amish," Amanda muttered. Naomi elbowed her in the ribs. Amanda shot her an irritated look, but didn't say anything else.

Benjamin stepped forward. "What is that supposed to mean? I did hear that, you know."

"Nothing," Naomi cut in. She glared at Amanda, then focused on their big sister. "Right, Miriam?"

Miriam raised an eyebrow before turning her back to Benjamin and picking up the serving spoon beside the stove. Her expression had not been very comforting.

"Look, I know you're keeping something from me. I may be your little brother, but it's about time you stopped treating me like I'm still a *kinner*. Or have you forgotten that I'm nearly twenty-one? And I'm only twenty-seven minutes younger than Leah."

"If you have to remind us of your age, there's probably a reason," Amanda said.

Benjamin rolled his eyes.

"Twenty-seven minutes is a long time," Leah said and winked at Benjamin.

"Stop trying to change the subject," Benjamin said, but he shot her a smile.

Naomi shook her head. "It's wrong to gossip."

Benjamin's smile disappeared and he threw up

his hands. "Then why are you all talking about it—whatever *it* is?"

"That's different. It's not gossip when it's just us."

"Yeah, I don't think that's how it works. And anyway, why wouldn't *us* include me?"

"Because you're our brother. It's different."

"You're really not going to tell me what's going on with Emma, are you?"

Leah stopped wiping the counter. She set down the dish towel and folded it slowly. "Benjamin," she said softly, "it's best you let this conversation go. I'm sorry we were talking in front of you. I know you and Emma have always been friends, but you probably won't be seeing her anytime soon. It's best to just let her be for now."

"Why won't you just come out and tell me what's going on?"

Leah looked conflicted. She shook her head and slid the dish towel to the back of the counter. "It isn't my story to tell. I'm sorry."

Benjamin studied Leah for a moment. He didn't like how uncomfortable she looked. His chest tightened at the thought that something might be wrong with Emma. "Now I'm worried." He met her eyes with a hard, steady gaze. "Should I be?"

Leah sighed. "*Ya.* I'm afraid so."

Benjamin stared at her for a moment, but he

knew she wasn't going to say anything else. He sighed, pulled open the kitchen door, dodged a chicken, and marched into the bright sunlight. He squinted and headed for the goat barn. With every step, he thought of Emma and wondered what was wrong. His mind swung from one bad scenario to another. By the time he reached the barn, Benjamin knew he had to stop tormenting himself. If he had one talent, it was thinking of the worst possible outcome. He had a wonderful imagination that way. If only he could be as skilled at everything else in life. He had been born with developmental coordination disorder, also known as dyspraxia, so he tended to be a little slower to get his jobs done, less coordinated than everyone else around him. It affected his vision too—mainly depth perception and tracking—but because it was neurological, glasses didn't help. He also had learning disabilities, which was common for people with the disorder. None of this affected his intelligence. He was as smart as his sisters, but he didn't always come across that way.

It was all subtle enough that most people outside of his family didn't even know, but that almost made it worse because people sometimes assumed that he was careless or lazy. No one knew how much that hurt. No one but his twin, Leah, who took the time to listen. And Emma, because he had been able to share his feelings with her when they were growing up. She had always been that good a friend. His best friend, really. She had even pointed out that God made him Amish to make the burden lighter. "No one knows you can't ride a bike or drive a car because we're not allowed," she had said once. "Clyde can pretty much drive our buggy for me," he responded, referring to their reliable old horse. They had both laughed at the time, but the idea stuck with him. He wished he could see Emma right now and tell her he was thinking of her.

When Benjamin reached the barn, he paused and gazed across the east field. He adjusted his straw hat to shield his eyes from the glare of the sun. Beyond the grass and scattered wildflowers lay the Yoder property—and Emma. He wondered what she was doing right now.

The goats bleated from their pen and Benjamin remembered that he needed to stay on task. "I'm coming, *ya*?" He pushed open the door to the weathered building and grabbed the feed bucket to provide the extra nutrients and vitamins the dairy goats needed to keep up production. The unpainted wooden boards gave the structure an old-fashioned, rustic feel that Benjamin liked. It seemed like the way a farm should look, even if the barn wasn't red like most people envisioned one should be.

Movement in the corner of his eye caught Benjamin's attention and he stopped, then spun around to see a goat prancing across the yard without a care in the world. "Hey!" he shouted before muttering, "Not again." Lilli had a habit of escaping. Well, to be honest, Benjamin had a habit of neglecting to latch the gate to the goat pen. He had to catch her before his sisters found out. They would never let him forget. Or worse, they would just look at him with that pitying expression as if he would never quite be on their level.

Benjamin took off toward Lilli. "Come on back, girl! You need to take your vitamins before you go out to graze, ain't so?" Lilli stared at him for a moment before darting away, toward the Yoder farm. Benjamin groaned and picked up his speed. Just before Lilli crossed the property line, she glanced back at him with an expression that looked an awful lot like glee. Benjamin just knew that Lilli was enjoying this.

As he followed her into the Yoder field, Benjamin tripped over a clump of dirt and almost fell, but managed to right himself. He jogged down the hill after Lilli, then watched her head straight for Edna Yoder's vegetable garden. Of course. Where else would a goat go? He forced himself to sprint the remaining few yards. The last thing he wanted was to knock on the bishop's door with a half-eaten head of cabbage in his hand and admit what happened. Of course, it might not be so bad if Emma answered the door instead of Edna. She would probably think the situation was hilarious. But Emma might not be the one to answer the door.

Benjamin watched as Lilli buried her head in the cabbage patch. She was going to tear it apart fast. His lungs burned, but he pushed himself to keep running. He was almost there. Then, just as he careened into the garden, Emma rounded the corner of the house, coming out of nowhere. His heart bobbed right into his throat and he skidded to a stop, barely in time to keep from bumping into her. "Emma! I heard you were back! My sisters said—"

Benjamin stopped talking. Emma was staring at him. She didn't look happy to see him at all. Benjamin frowned. "I'm sorry. I didn't startle you, did I? My goat got into the garden and I just..." Benjamin didn't like the look on Emma's face. It was an unreadable mix of stress, frustration, and anger. Her green eyes were wide and they did not have their usual sparkle. Instead, they seemed dull and listless behind her expression of shock. Her cheeks had lost their rosy color. And her skin seemed pale. She had always loved the sun and he had never seen her without a tan.

He backed away a step and lowered his voice. "Are you okay? I didn't mean to…" He wanted to reach out and take her hand, but he didn't, of course. He just wished he could do something to fix whatever was wrong. "Did I…do something? I mean, besides almost bumping into you? I'm really sorry about that. I know I startled you. But, uh…" He looked away and scratched his jaw. "It's really *gut* to see you again." He looked back at her and saw her hand drift down to her belly. His eyes followed her hand and he noticed a round bulge beneath her purple cape dress. It took his mind a moment to register what he was seeing.

A baby bump.

Benjamin froze. He had no idea what to say. His eyes flicked back up to hers and he understood the expression on her face now.

Emma stared back for a moment, then shook her head, turned around, and fled.

Emma couldn't believe what just happened. She had never felt so ashamed. Well, that wasn't quite true. The last few months had been nothing but shame. Oh sure, she had repented, returned to the faith, and been baptized. And plenty of people had welcomed her back with open arms.

But not all. And those hard stares and smug whispers had just about broken her. The worst thing was that she couldn't help but feel she deserved the condemnation.

To avoid that shame back home, her family had sent her to stay with her uncle in Lancaster County as the due date approached. She could live here until they figured out what to do with her and the new baby. Emma didn't want to think about that—she was taking things one day at a time and didn't have a plan yet. For now, she was hiding from everyone she knew back in Holmes County, Ohio. She had planned on hiding from everyone in Bluebird Hills too.

It was too late for that now.

Emma's chest burned and her cheeks felt hot. Of all the people to run into—almost literally— why did it have to be Benjamin Stoltzfus? They had been good friends until they'd drifted apart while she was on her *Rumspringa*. That was when she had stopped spending her summers next door to him, staying back home in Ohio and getting into trouble instead. Benjamin had not strayed like she had. He had always been good and true to the faith, the way she wished she had been. She could never live up to his standards. She had seen the look on his face when he noticed that she was expecting. He had been shocked and disappointed. Before that, he had frowned at her. Maybe he had already known. She tried to remember everything he had said. Didn't he say he was happy to see her? He was probably just trying to be nice. That was the way Benjamin was. He would be kind no matter what, even if he didn't want to be.

Emma glanced over her shoulder. No sign of Benjamin. He wasn't following her. Of course he wasn't. He would want to put as much distance between them as possible. She hurried past the wheelbarrow and chicken coop, took the porch steps as fast as she could, and flung open the front door. Aunt Edna poked her head out of the kitchen doorway. "You got the carrots for the potpie?" Her gray hair was tucked beneath a starched *kapp* and there was a sprinkle of white flour on the apron covering her plump midsection.

Emma froze. "*Nee.* I'll go back and pick them. But not right now. Can you give me a minute?"

Edna's usually cheerful face crinkled. "Are you okay? Did you forget what you went outside to do? I've heard that—" Edna cut herself off and Emma knew that she had been about to say something about how women who are expecting have trouble remembering things. But neither of them had actually come right out and addressed Emma's situation. She had only arrived that morning and had not even seen her uncle Amos. He had gone to a horse auction with some other men from their church district and wasn't back yet.

"*Ya*, I'm okay. I just…"

The crease in Edna's forehead deepened. "You look like you've seen a ghost."

Emma hesitated. "*Vell*, it feels that way."

Edna stared at her for a moment. "I think we need a *gut* cup of tea, *ya*?"

"Oh. Um…" Emma's gaze moved to the staircase that led to the guest bedroom upstairs. "I was just going to my room for a minute…" All she wanted was to bury herself beneath the Jacob's ladder quilt on the guest bed and pretend none of this was happening.

"I'll put on the kettle. How about a nice lemon herbal tea? *Gut* for stress, I hear. And no caffeine." With that, Edna began to gently steer Emma toward the front door. "Let's sit on the porch. I'll bring it to you."

Emma went rigid, forcing Edna to stop short. She bounced against Emma and stumbled to regain her balance.

"Sorry!" Emma said. "But I can't…"

Edna raised her eyebrows. "I see."

Emma wondered if she did.

"We can sit inside." Edna motioned toward the living room. "I'll be there in a minute."

Emma settled onto the couch while she waited

for Edna. The space had always felt snug and comforting, with her aunt's handmade quilt folded on the back of the couch and another hanging from the quilt rack. The black potbellied stove filled the air with the scent of wood smoke, and a view of the orchard lay beyond the windows. It was as if nothing had changed since the last summer that she had been here.

If only that were true.

The seconds ticked by in time with the thud of her heartbeat. She dreaded what Edna might say—what she thought of her now. Edna bustled into the living room a few minutes later with a tray in her hands. She set down a cup of tea and a plate of chocolate chip cookies on the coffee table in front of Emma before sitting down in her wicker rocking chair.

An uncomfortable silence filled the room. Emma tried to focus on her tea. She picked up the familiar cream-colored mug and blew across the top. Lemon-scented steam curled into her face.

"So," Edna said. "You're avoiding Benjamin."

Emma straightened in her chair. "What do you mean?" Of all the things that Edna would say first, this was not what Emma had expected.

Edna opened her mouth to respond when the front door opened, then slammed shut. "Hello!" came a cheerful shout from the entry hall, followed by footsteps across the hardwood floor. Amos appeared in the doorway with a wide grin on his face. He had always resembled a jovial gnome with his wizened features, small frame, and bald head. Emma's heart leaped at the sight of his smile. He had always made her feel loved and welcome. Maybe that hadn't changed, after all.

Amos crossed the room in an instant to pull Emma into a big hug. "Can't tell you how *gut* it is to have you here," he said.

Emma tried to return his smile. But she was too surprised and overwhelmed. "Really?"

Amos looked serious for a moment, but his smile returned quickly. "*Ya*, of course. You're our Emma. Nothing will change that."

Emma swallowed hard. She felt the shame deep in her belly, like a stone. "Nothing?"

"Nothing," Edna and Amos said at the same time.

"Oh." Emma didn't know what else to say.

A knock on the door kept her from having to respond. Amos and Edna glanced at one another. "Right on time," he said.

Edna tried to smother a short burst of laughter. "Now, be nice, Amos."

"Wait, who's here? Did you invite someone?" Emma's heart galloped into her throat at the thought that it might be Benjamin.

"*Nee*, we didn't invite anyone," Amos said. "But it doesn't take a genius to guess who would show up at our door as soon as you arrive. I'm surprised I beat her here."

A slow, sinking realization came over Emma. "Viola Esch," she murmured.

"She means well," Edna said.

Viola Esch had a talent for being the first to find out—and spread—any news. "Can we please pretend not to be home?" If Viola found out why Emma was here, everyone would know soon.

Amos and Edna exchanged a quick glance. Then Edna shook her head. "No use putting off the inevitable. You can't hide away forever."

"Oh, I don't… I mean, why not?"

Amos and Edna both frowned. They didn't need to answer because Emma's question was unrealistic and she knew it. But still…

Edna stood up to answer the door, but after another hard knock, they heard it swing open. "Amos?" Viola said loudly enough to reach them. "I saw you pulling in a minute ago. Hello?"

Edna sighed and sat back down. "Come on in, Viola. We're in the living room."

They heard the shuffle of feet and a cane tapping the hardwood floor, then Viola marched into the living room with a cake tin tucked beneath her free arm. "I've brought a hummingbird cake." She moved quickly for a woman in her nineties. "Now, where is she?" Viola's attention shot straight to Emma. "Ah, there you are." She set the cake tin down on the coffee table and adjusted her glasses. "How far along are you?"

Emma balked. Amos cleared his throat.

"No use wasting time on small talk," Viola said.

"No," Edna said quietly, "I suppose not."

Emma squeezed her eyes shut to try to escape. "A little over eight months."

"Hmm."

Emma could feel Viola watching her and she opened her eyes. "How did you know?"

Viola hobbled over to the empty side of the couch and dropped onto it. "Ah, feels *gut* to sit down, ain't so? Not as young as I used to be, you know."

Everyone stared at Viola, waiting for the answer. She propped her cane against the arm of the couch and smoothed the front of her emerald green cape dress. "I was down at Beiler's Quilt and Fabric Shop, talking to Betty Beiler."

Edna shifted in her seat. Emma caught the look on her aunt's face as she realized that she had not been clever enough to evade Viola.

"I asked Betty how the shop was doing—you know how bad sales have been since that Sew N Save opened up across town. Although who would want to shop there, I couldn't imagine.

Nothing but cheap polyesters in worldly colors and teenagers working there who won't even say hello and—"

"You were telling us about what Betty said," Edna interrupted.

"Right. Betty told me she had just moved a lot of stock and I asked what kind of stock and who bought it and she told me. And, of course, it's been around town that Emma was coming back, even though it isn't summertime. Well, why else would you have been buying fabric that everyone knows is used to make *boppli* blankets and *boppli* clothes?"

Edna let out a long, slow breath. She had a look of defeat on her face.

"I've heard the rest from my third cousin over in Sugarcreek, Ohio. The *unfortunate Rumspringa*, and all that." "But now that Emma's come back to the faith and been baptized, that's all forgiven. So, it's time to get down to business. There isn't any time to waste, not with Emma eight months gone." Viola pointed her chin toward the cake tin on the coffee table. "Although there is time for cake. How about cutting us some slices, *ya*? And I'll have a cup of *kaffi* with mine. You know how I like it."

"*Ya,*" Edna said. "I certainly do."

"Viola, what do you mean about not wasting time?" Amos cut in.

"*Vell*, we only have a few weeks to find a *gut* Amish *daed* for this *boppli*."

Emma stiffened. "*Ach, nee*. That isn't… I'm not going to…" She shook her head. "This *boppli* isn't going to have a *daed*." She could feel the heat prickle across her skin and overtake her face. She looked down and wished she could sink into the floor.

"Nonsense. You've got a perfectly *gut* candidate right next door." Viola waved toward the neighboring farm. "Benjamin Stoltzfus may be too shy to have courted anyone yet, but he's a *gut* boy. He'll make a fine *daed*. And the two of you have been friends for years." Viola gave a firm nod. "It's a *gut* match."

Amos and Edna exchanged a look.

"*Nee*. Benjamin isn't…" Emma turned her attention to her aunt and uncle, desperate for them to stop the conversation. "He would never want to marry me."

Amos looked sad. He didn't have the usual twinkle in his eyes and the lines on his face seemed deeper. Edna's hands moved nervously across the hem of her apron. She picked at a loose thread, then shook her head and stood up. "I'll serve the cake, *ya*?"

"Let's send for Benjamin," Viola said. "He can have cake and *kaffi* with us." She motioned toward Emma. "Give them a chance to chat."

Emma stood up so fast it made her dizzy. *"Nee!"* She staggered forward a step. "I can't. I have to…" Her mind raced for an excuse. Any excuse. "I have to pick carrots! It's urgent. Aunt Edna has to get the potpie on and she's waiting on them. Right, Aunt Edna?" Emma didn't give Edna a chance to answer. She shot out of the room so fast that not even Viola had time to stop her.

Chapter Two

Benjamin wondered what to do. Emma clearly didn't want to see him and he wanted to respect her wishes. But his heart longed to connect with her again, even just as friends. He was okay with that. She was worth knowing whether or not she was interested in him romantically. She had always been so much fun, with her vibrant personality and booming laugh. Sure, she had always tended to get into a little bit of trouble here and there—his sisters used to complain that she was a bad influence—but it was all in good fun. There was the incident when they let the goats loose in the house, or when they made mud puddles in the front yard so his sisters would get their shoes dirty when they fed the chickens, or the time they sled down the hill that led up to the south pasture, slammed right into the milking shed, and broke the door wide open.

But this time, Emma was in real trouble. And he wanted to help her. But what could he possibly do? At the very least he could be a good listener. That had always been easy for him. He liked listening better than talking. There was less pressure that way.

Benjamin mixed the vitamins into the goat feed, poured the mixture into the trough, and reached down to pat one of the Angoras. "That's a *gut* girl," he murmured. The soft, white fleece felt good between his fingers. Another goat bumped the back of his knee and he hopped to the side, then tripped over Lilli before he caught himself. He straightened up, dusted off his pants, and gave her a stern look. "Stay put, *ya*? No more running away." She stared at him with an impish gleam in her eye before turning her attention to the feed trough. He shook his head and walked away, swinging the empty feed bucket in his hand.

Dust rose in the distance and he watched as a buggy wound its way up the gravel driveway. He strode out of the pen and made it twenty paces before he got a funny feeling that he was forgetting something. He doubled back and latched the gate, gave a satisfied nod, then headed to the driveway.

Pretty soon, he could make out Viola Esch in the buggy. He sighed and waited. There was no use trying to run. "*Ah*, just who I wanted to see," Viola shouted as soon as she drew close enough for her voice to carry. Benjamin sighed. Of course she had come to see him. "Whoa." She tugged the reins and the buggy shuddered to a stop. The horse gave an irritated whinny and shook his head, sending the mane rippling.

"I've just *kumme* from the Yoders."

Benjamin straightened up at that. "You did?"

"Just said so, didn't I?"

Benjamin frowned.

"Anyway, I'm sure you know that Emma is staying there now."

Benjamin nodded.

"*Vell*, she needs *gut* fresh milk. And goat's milk has lots of vitamins, ain't so?"

"For certain sure. That's why the *Englischers* buy it."

"And yours is all pasteurized? Emma can't risk getting sick."

"We only sell pasteurized milk. We wouldn't risk getting anybody sick."

"*Gut.*" Viola gave a decisive nod. "*Vell*, hurry up, then."

Benjamin's frown deepened.

"Don't just stand there, get some milk over to Emma. The sooner the better."

"Oh. Right." He rubbed the back of his neck. "I've got some wood to chop, so I might just send one of my sisters."

"*Nee.*"

"I, uh, I'm not so sure that she wants to see me."

"Nonsense. I was just over there."

Benjamin's heart leaped. "Did she say that she wanted to see me?"

"She said enough. Now get on over there."

Benjamin didn't find that response very reassuring. But before he could say anything else, Viola slapped the reins. "Walk on." The buggy took off and Benjamin was left to watch the trail of dust and wonder what on earth he was going to say to Emma if he actually paid her a visit. He stood there for a moment, considering. Well, goat's milk would be good for her and the baby, that much was true. It was the right thing to do. And if she didn't want to see him, she could take the milk and tell him to leave. At least she would have the milk to drink, regardless.

As he walked to the main production building, his mind began to wander. He thought about how nice it would be to give Emma's baby something soft made from Angora wool. Stoneybrook Farm raised Angora goats for fiber and Alpine and Saanen goats for milk. He considered the gifts he had to offer as he pushed open the door and breathed in the cool, damp air of the dairy. His boots thudded across the concrete floor as he walked past the diesel-powered processing equipment. His distorted reflection moved across the shiny silver surface of one of the big metal vats. He heard the door to the industrial propone-powered refrigerator open and close with a muffled thump. He hoped it wasn't Amanda or Miriam. They had always been the most critical of Emma. He rounded the corner and saw both of them standing beside the refrigerators. Amanda had a clipboard and pencil in her hands, while Miriam unloaded a cart of glass bottles filled with white, frothy milk.

"Hey," he said. "I'll just grab a few of those, okay?"

"Uh…" Amanda flipped a page on her clipboard and tapped it with the end of her pencil. "Most of these are for an order." She flipped another page. "But you can take two bottles from the bottom rack of the cart." She looked up from the clipboard. "You've never been much of a milk drinker. What's it for?"

"Oh, *vell*, you know."

"No, we don't know," Miriam said. "That's why we're asking."

"Just being a good neighbor." Benjamin looked down at the floor and kicked at a crack in the concrete.

Amanda's eyes narrowed. "Which neighbor, exactly?"

"Um…"

"We've already gone over this, Benji." Miriam paused to put down the milk bottle in her hand. The glass clinked against the metal shelf. "It's best not to go over to the Yoders for a while."

"Emma needs milk."

Miriam exhaled. "Right."

"She does."

"I know, that's why I said, 'right.'"

"*Vell*, it wasn't a very enthusiastic 'right.'"

There was an awkward silence.

"I can't believe you have a problem with me taking milk to a neighbor who needs it. We're Amish. We take care of our own."

"Of course we do." Amanda set the clipboard down on top of the cart. "I'll take it to her."

"*Nee.* I'll take it." Benjamin had been worried about facing Emma, but now that his sisters were trying to stop him, it made him realize how right it felt to see her again. It was always easier to give in to his sisters than to argue with them, but this time he would stand his ground. He wouldn't let them keep him from doing what he knew was right. Emma had always been his friend, not theirs.

"No need." Amanda bent down and pulled two bottles of milk from the cart. "I'll take care of it right now."

"Nee." Benjamin grabbed two of his own bottles and turned on his heels. "She's *my* friend."

He could hear one of them sigh as he strode away. *"Ya,"* Miriam murmured. "That's the problem."

Benjamin pretended not to hear. He had enough to worry about as it was. Could he really face Emma after their encounter earlier today? What was he going to say? *Hello, Emma, I know you don't want to see me, but here I am anyway?* This was not going to go well.

He clutched the milk bottles tightly as he made his way across the farmyard. He had a tendency to drop things and the last thing he wanted was to have to face his sisters again and admit that he was back for more milk. Their Anatolian shepherd, Ollie, trotted over and sniffed at the bottles.

"Where were you when Lilli got out today?"

Ollie looked at him with his expressive brown eyes.

"Must have been busy keeping the coyote and foxes away, ain't so?" Benjamin tucked one of the milk bottles under his arm so he could free up a hand to pet Ollie's neck. At 150 pounds, the guard dog was tall enough that Benjamin didn't have to stoop very far. He could feel the muscles that roped beneath the short brindle coat. "Don't follow me, okay. You'll scare the Yoders' cat."

Ollie wagged his tail before loping off, toward the barn. They had never lost a kid since they got him. He was a good dog, but he was reserved and aloof; a working dog, not a pet.

Benjamin had always appreciated how close the Yoder farmhouse was, but the walk felt too short today. He still had no idea what to say to Emma. She might not even be willing to see him. He made his way down the grassy hill, past the gravel driveway, and skirted the rows of vegetables in the side yard. He could feel his face heat up as he rounded the house and stepped onto the front porch. He passed the rocking chairs where he and Emma used to drink lemonade on hot summer afternoons, took a deep breath, and knocked on the door.

He could hear mumbled voices inside the house followed by heavy footsteps. He shifted his weight from one leg to the other. This was a bad idea. Maybe he should have let Amanda bring the milk. Emma probably wouldn't even let him in the house. She had made it very clear that she didn't want to see him. He set the bottles onto the doormat and turned away. He would just leave the milk and go. He made it to the edge of the porch when he heard the door swing open.

"Benjamin?" Bishop Amos's voice.

Benjamin turned around. "Hi. I was just, uh, dropping off some milk. You know, for Emma."

"Ah."

Benjamin stared at Amos for a moment.

"Running off pretty quick, *ya*?"

"*Ach, vell*, there's wood to chop…"

"There's always wood to chop." Amos motioned him inside. "Come on in. We were just having some hummingbird cake. There's plenty left and there's still some *kaffi* in the carafe."

"But…"

Amos raised his eyebrows.

Benjamin didn't finish the sentence. "Okay. *Danki*. That sounds *abbeditlich*."

"It *is* delicious." Amos winked. "I already had two slices." He patted his slim stomach. "*Gut* thing I can afford it." Amos had always been small boned. His wife was taller and plumper, which only made Amos seem even smaller.

Benjamin knew there was no way to politely get out of going inside. Part of him was relieved that he had no choice but to see Emma. Part of him wanted to run away and never come back. Emma must have felt the same way, because as soon as she saw Benjamin the color drained from her face. She stumbled up from the couch, gripping the arm for support as she grappled with the extra weight she carried in her midsection. "Benjamin?" Her eyes shot to Edna, then to Amos.

"Hello." Benjamin wanted to take back the

word as soon as he said it. It didn't seem the right response. But what else could he say?

"I've got to see to the potpie," Emma said.

"Ach, nee." Edna stood up and put a hand on Emma's shoulder. "I've got that, dear. You sit back down and have another cup of tea."

Emma looked to Amos with panic in her eyes.

Amos ran his fingers through his long, white beard. He looked uncertain now that he saw Emma's reaction.

"I need help with the stove, remember?" Edna said.

"The stove?"

Edna stepped toward him and nudged him in his side with her elbow. *"Ya.* The propane line. Remember?"

"Ah! *Ya.* Of course. The propane line." He bolted toward the door. "Right away, dear."

And just like that, the room cleared out and Benjamin was left alone with Emma. She hesitated, then dropped back down onto the couch. Her expression was guarded. "I didn't tell them to do that," she said.

The words stung. Emma was making it clear that she didn't want to be alone with him. *"Nee,* I didn't think you did." He hovered awkwardly. "I didn't even mean to *kumme* in. I was just dropping off some milk." When she didn't respond, Benjamin felt the need to keep talking. "I, uh, tried to just leave it on the porch, but you know how it is."

"*Ya*. My aunt and uncle won't let anyone leave without feeding them."

"*Ya*." Benjamin stood for another moment. The clock on the wall ticked in the silence. "Do you mind if I sit down?"

"*Nee*, of course not." Her tone and face didn't match her words, though. "Sit down and have some cake. Viola Esch made it, so you know it's *gut*."

"Oh, that explains it."

"Explains what?"

"*Vell*, Viola must have *kumme* by my place right after she left here. She told me to bring the milk."

Something flickered behind Emma's eyes. She looked away and her shoulders sagged a little bit more than before. "So that's why you came over."

Benjamin was thankful for the save. Since she didn't want him here, it was best to let her know that Viola had insisted he come. It was true, after all, even if it wasn't the whole truth. "*Ya*," he said. "She made sure of it."

Emma's eyes moved back up to his. There was something achingly vulnerable in her expression. He had never seen that look on her face before. She was normally so sure of herself. He was looking at the same honey-blond hair, the same green eyes, and the same heart-shaped face and button nose, but this was not the same Emma.

"Was that the only reason?" she asked.

Benjamin didn't know how to answer. He had to think carefully. "Just being a *gut* neighbor." It seemed the best response. He wasn't admitting that he wanted to see her, but he wasn't denying it, either. Even so, it had been the wrong answer. He knew because a flash of emotion passed over Emma's face before she turned away to stare into her mug of tea, as if he wasn't even there.

He shouldn't have come inside.

Chapter Three

⁓

Emma wanted to disappear. Maybe if she tried hard enough to pretend none of this was happening, it would all just go away.

But of course, life didn't work like that. She listened to Benjamin's foot tapping the floor as she gripped the warm mug between her fingers. A long minute passed, then another. Why didn't Benjamin leave? It was clear that he didn't want to be there. He had practically said so. If Viola hadn't pushed him into it, he would never have bothered to come over.

She watched him out of the corner of her eye. He slumped in his chair as he turned his mug in his hands. Then his deep, brown eyes cut to hers. Emma's throat tightened. He had caught her staring at him. She should look away. But for an instant she felt locked in place, unable to tear her gaze from his. His eyes had always been so expressive, so kind. And now they were pulling her in and she didn't want to resist. His face was so familiar with its high cheekbones, straight nose, and full lips. She had always been so comfortable alongside him. Once upon a time, Benjamin had understood her. And now, as their eyes connected, it almost felt as if he did again.

But no. He had already made himself clear. Emma dropped her eyes and adjusted the skirt of her dress. The rustle of the starched fabric sounded too loud in the quiet room. Benjamin cleared his throat and stood up. "*Vell*, guess I best be getting on. There's wood to chop."

Emma cringed inside. Benjamin used to always say that he had wood to chop when he wanted to get out of something. It was his catch-all phrase. And since there was always wood to chop, it wasn't technically a lie. But she was certain that he had no intention of racing home in order to pick up an ax and get to work.

She felt herself crumpling inside. Her only friend in Bluebird Hills didn't want anything to do with her. She had feared that would happen. In fact, it had been on her mind throughout the long, lonely bus ride from Ohio. She had ruminated on it as she stared out the grimy window, watching the bleak, gray sky and the endless stretch of black pavement. But she had held out hope that Benjamin would understand, somehow. That he would be different from her friends back home who gave strained smiles to her face, then turned around and whispered behind her back. She had repented.

She had come back to the faith. There was nothing more she could do. But that didn't seem to matter to them. It must not matter to Benjamin, either. He wasn't who she had thought he was. Emma sighed. "*Oll recht. Danki* for the milk." It took all of her strength to hold in her emotions and keep her expression even. She would not let him know how much his rejection hurt.

Especially since she was still reeling from Liam's rejection. She thought that she had been in love with the father of her baby. Everything had felt brighter and more exciting around him. But now she realized it had just been a *Rumspringa* crush, heightened by the thrill of the unknown. There had been no foundation, no friendship beneath the surface. He had been handsome, fun, and charming. Nothing more. But she had naively fallen for all of it. Until he claimed their baby wasn't his and disappeared from her life.

Now, she was alone.

Well, that wasn't entirely true. She had her aunt and uncle, thankfully. But she didn't have a best friend. She didn't have anyone who truly, deeply understood her, whom she could laugh or cry with. Benjamin had been all those things, once.

When Emma looked up again, Benjamin was gone.

Emma escaped to her room for the evening as

soon as she could. But the whitewashed walls, blue braided rug, and narrow bed didn't feel comforting and familiar as they once had. Neither did the old sampler that Edna had framed and hung on the wall years ago. It had the ABCs, numbers one through ten, an image of a one-room schoolhouse, and a Bible verse embroidered on it. Beneath the sampler sat the wooden chest that she had brought with her from Ohio. It held everything she owned and Emma wondered how long it would stay in this room. Was there any future for her beyond these four walls?

She sat down on the edge of the bed and stared out the window until the orchard trees faded into black silhouettes and the pink sky eased into darkness. After that, she could only see her own reflection in the glass. Somewhere, on the neighboring farm, Benjamin was beneath the same sky, wrapped in the same darkness. She wondered if he was thinking of her.

No, that was silly. He had his own life now. They had not been close for several years. And besides, why did she care? They had only ever been friends. Why did it matter if he were thinking of her or not? Something vague and soft tugged at her from deep within her heart. Viola's words repeated in her mind. *He'll make a fine daed.* Emma sighed and stared into the shadows beyond the window. "*Ya*, I'm sure he would," she murmured. He had always been quiet and kind, slow to speak and quick to listen. But he wasn't interested in her. That was clear. Emma just wished that Viola could see that. It would be humiliating if she pushed a match and Benjamin had to reject Emma outright, rather than just hinting at it.

Emma felt a deep fatigue that weighed down her mind and not just her body. She lay back on the bed without changing into her white cotton nightgown. She pulled up the Jacob's ladder quilt from the foot of the bed to cover her, but she still felt cold inside. The wind whistled outside her window, whispering that she was all alone. Her hand moved to her belly. Soon she would have someone to cuddle and love. But how would she manage it all on her own?

When Emma woke up the next morning, still fully dressed, she couldn't remember falling asleep. She glanced at the window and saw that the sun was higher in the sky than it should be. She had overslept. Emma hurried out of bed and splashed cold water from the washbasin onto her face. She quickly pulled off her *kapp*, unpinned her long, honey-blond hair, brushed it out, and put it back up in a tight bun. She studied her *kapp* for a moment. It was winkled from where she had slept in it. She looked down and saw that her dress was wrinkled as well. Well, there was nothing to be done about it. She tried to smooth the wrinkles out the best she could, pinned her *kapp* in place, and hurried downstairs.

Edna was bustling around the kitchen. The smell of biscuits, gravy, and coffee lingered in the cozy room. "Ah!" Edna smiled when she saw Emma standing in the doorway. "I was just about to go wake you up."

"I'm sorry I slept late."

"We knew you needed your rest. But now we've got to get going—"

"Buggy's hitched up and we're all ready!" came a cheerful shout from down the hall, followed by footsteps. Amos popped into the kitchen and grinned when he saw Emma. "Ah, *gut*. Let's go."

Emma glanced from Amos to Edna with a confused expression.

"Silas Hochstetler paid us a visit early this morning. You know those old maple trees in their yard? One of them fell on the barn during the night. Forecast is calling for rain tomorrow so we've got to get a new roof on right away. I've already sent out word that we're having a work frolic today." Silas had recently married Mary King and moved his harness-making business into her little white barn.

"Oh." Emma froze. Surely they didn't expect her to come with them.

"I've packed you some breakfast to go." Edna grabbed a wicker basket from the counter and began to steer Emma toward the door.

"Ach, nee," Emma said, even as her feet moved in the direction that she did not want them to go. "I'll stay here and have dinner ready when you *kumme* back. And I can get some cleaning done. And tend the garden."

Edna did not stop steering her toward the door. She and Amos exchanged a quick look. Amos cleared his throat. "*Vell*, as the bishop, it wouldn't do for me not to bring my family to help, ain't so?"

"Oh." Emma's stomach sank. He was right. They couldn't go without her. What would people think?

But what would people think if she *did* show up?

Emma swallowed hard. They had almost reached the front door. "I, uh, maybe you could explain that I'm not feeling well?"

Edna and Amos both paused. They made eye contact again, then Edna nodded at Amos. She put a gentle hand on Emma's shoulder. "Emma, I know this is hard for you. But you can't hide forever. You're going to have to face the community sometime."

"Now's as *gut* a time as any, ain't so?" Amos's voice was kind, but the words still cut through Emma.

"I thought maybe, we could wait until after..." Her voice faded away.

"You can't stay shut up in the house for weeks," Edna said.

"Oh, *vell*, I think that I can." In fact, Emma was positive she could.

"*Ach*, Emma." Amos shook his head. "You have a right to be a part of the community. Everything's forgiven now. You confessed, came back to the Amish, and got baptized, remember?"

"*Ya*, but..." She looked down at her feet, but realized she couldn't see them anymore. She stared at the round bulge beneath her cape dress instead. "Not everyone will see it that way."

"That's true, I'm afraid. But it doesn't make them right." Amos gave her a firm, steady look. "The ones who accept you, they're the ones in the right."

Emma wanted to point out that knowing they were wrong only made it marginally better. The shame would still be there, whether or not it was justified. But Emma didn't get a chance to say anything else. Amos and Edna had bustled her out to the buggy before she could think of another excuse.

Emma had always enjoyed visiting Mary

King—Mary Hochstetler now. But Emma had not seen Mary since she'd been married. And now, for the first time, she dreaded seeing the white clapboard house with its cute dormer windows and the small, tidy yard lined with maple trees. Mary lived near Bluebird Hills' downtown area so it took a while for the buggy to wind its way down the country back roads, past the red barns and silver silos, the golden wheat fields waving in the breeze, and the green pastures dotted with Holstein cows. But eventually, the inevitable happened and Mary's little white house appeared in the distance. Emma's belly tightened. At first she thought it was her baby kicking and she put a hand across her baby bump. But then she realized it was the dread taking hold of her body. Her heart began to pound and she felt a wild need to jump from the bench seat and run. It didn't matter where. She just needed to run as far and as fast as she could. Everything in her body was shouting at her to do it.

Instead, she gripped her hands together until the knuckles turned white and she forced herself to stay in the buggy, even though her heart kicked against her ribs and her pulse thudded in her ears.

"Looks like we've already got a *gut* turnout," Amos said from the front seat.

"Word travels fast on the Amish telegraph," Edna said.

Yes, Emma thought. But she wasn't thinking of the damaged barn.

Amos clicked his tongue and steered the dappled gray buggy horse into the yard. Emma got a good view of the barn and the maple tree lying atop its roof. She told herself that she should care more about what the Hochstetlers were going through than about her problems. They might lose business over this. And someone could have been hurt, although thankfully, nobody was. But all Emma could think about was her own problems. And that made her feel even more ashamed of herself.

"Whoa," Amos murmured and tugged the reins. The buggy lurched to a sudden stop and Emma bounced against the back of the bench seat. She waited as Amos and Edna slid out of the buggy, even though she knew she couldn't hide inside much longer. That would just make her look even worse. She counted to five in her head. *One. Two. Three. Four. Five.* And then she forced herself to climb down, into the bright sunlight and crowded yard.

Amos appeared beside the buggy to take her hand and help her navigate the drop. After that, he was whisked away into the group of men who were planning the repairs. Emma looked up and saw the crowd staring at her. All the people she had grown up seeing during her summers in Bluebird Hills were there. And they were all looking at her. She felt her face flush. Her body felt hot and strange. The world began to feel woozy and distant. And her heart wouldn't stop pounding.

Then the whispers started. She was surrounded by staring faces who murmured to one another in low voices. She could only imagine what they were saying about her. She felt exposed and alone, even though she could feel Edna's hand on her elbow. "Just remember they're in the wrong if they don't accept you," Edna whispered. But her words were swallowed by the shame. It was all she could think or feel. It had begun to consume her.

But a deep, familiar voice stood out from the growing crowd. "Hey, Emma." Her attention shot to the back of the group. There was some shuffling and movement, then Benjamin emerged from among them and jogged toward her. He was wearing that big, goofy grin she had always loved and his eyes looked warm and bright. It was as if she had never left, as if they were friends again, just like they used to be. "*Gut* thing you could make it."

Emma felt the shame recede. Benjamin was here. He had come to rescue her.

* * *

Benjamin could not believe that everyone was standing and staring at Emma. It was inexcusable. He had seen the buggy pull into the yard and everything in him had tensed. He could only imagine what Emma was experiencing, the shame she must feel at facing the entire community. There was only one thing to do. He had to go to her side and stand with her. He would let her know that she wasn't alone.

As he jogged toward her, a pang of doubt flashed through him. She had made it clear that she didn't want him around. What if she didn't want to be seen with him in public? Was he making everything worse?

He had no choice. He wouldn't leave her on her own to face this crowd.

Benjamin watched Emma's face as he approached. Her features were so tight that it was hard to read them. But then, there was an unmistakable flicker of relief. She let out a long, shuddering breath and smiled at him. It was a weak smile, but it was real and it flooded him with warmth. He had done the right thing.

He reached her and stopped short. He had been jogging toward her pretty fast, so now it felt awkward to stop suddenly, with nothing to say or do. He could feel the eyes of the crowd on him, just as acutely as they had been on Emma.

"It's a *gut* day for a work frolic," he managed to say. It was the wrong thing and he felt embarrassed as soon as the words left his mouth, especially since he had said them loudly enough for everyone to hear. But he didn't know what else he could have said.

"Ya," Emma murmured. She looked down and studied the damp ground.

"Oll recht, let me through," Viola Esch said in a voice even louder than Benjamin's had been as she used her cane to part the crowd. "There she is." Viola hobbled over to Benjamin and Emma. "I can see no one else has anything better to do than stand around and gawk, but we know how to get down to work, ain't so?"

Benjamin wanted to hug good old Viola. She might be overbearing, but she was also great at defending people. And here she was, taking up for Emma.

Emma managed to nod, but said nothing. Benjamin could see that she was struggling to keep her bearings. She looked so vulnerable and alone. He wanted to make her see that she wasn't completely alone anymore—not as long as he was there. He would always be her friend. No matter what. But that wasn't something he could say to her. It would come out all wrong. He would just have to show her. It wouldn't be easy, but he would find a way, because he had to.

Viola pointed her cane at the crowd and began to dole out orders. Pretty soon, everyone was breaking off into smaller clumps as people headed toward their jobs. Benjamin took the opportunity to lean down, close to Emma's ear. "You *oll recht*?" He kept his voice low, so no one else could her.

She swallowed hard and stared at him for a moment. *"Ya,"* she murmured. "I am now."

Benjamin's heart leaped. He had made things better for her. He had made a difference. He grinned and she smiled. Her green eyes showed the smallest hint of their old sparkle and it gave him hope.

Then Viola was holding Emma's arm and marching her toward the house. *"Kumme,* there's cooking to get done. The menfolk will be hungry soon, ain't so?"

Benjamin took a moment to watch Emma walk away as a warm, happy feeling settled in his belly. Maybe he could keep making a difference for her.

"Benji, stop standing around." Benjamin hadn't realized that Amanda was hovering beside him, her hands on her hips. "You can help haul the timber." She hesitated and lowered her voice. "You can manage that, can't you?"

He frowned. "Of course I can."

She nodded and stared at him with an expression that Benjamin didn't like.

"What?" he asked. He glanced over at the barn, to where the other men were pulling apart the damaged roof.

"Don't try to work from the ladder or up on the roof. Stay on the ground."

"I'll be fine."

"You know you can't balance well enough. Don't take any risks."

"I said I'll be fine." He started to walk away, his mood spoiled. The rush of happiness had been replaced by the reminder that he was never quite good enough. It had been silly for him to think that he could have made a difference for Emma. She probably thought he wasn't good enough, either.

"Benji, wait."

Benjamin sighed and stopped. He turned around and scowled. "What?"

Amanda pursed her lips.

"What is it? I've got to stop standing around and help, remember?"

Amanda glanced at the crowd, and took a few quick steps toward Benjamin, until she was close enough to speak to him quietly. "That was *lecherich* to stand up for Emma like that. If you're not careful, the entire church district will think you want to court her."

"It isn't ridiculous to help a friend," Benjamin shot back. "And so what if everyone thinks I want to court her? What does that matter?"

Amanda sucked in her breath. She looked over his shoulder, then back to him. "*Vell*, you don't... Do you?"

"I told you, we're friends. We've only ever been friends."

Amanda opened her mouth, then clamped it shut and shook her head. "We'll talk more later. This isn't the place."

"Then you shouldn't have started it."

"I didn't. *You* did when you ran over to Emma like that."

Amanda shook her head and strode away. Benjamin stood alone on the lawn for a moment, wondering what he had started and what the consequences might be.

No matter what they were, he wasn't sorry.

Chapter Four

Mary Hochstetler waved Emma over as soon as she walked into the kitchen. Mary's dark gray eyes shone with new life since she had married Silas. A stab of loneliness speared Emma as she recognized Mary's transformation. Single until her midthirties, Mary had never been courted before she and Silas agreed to an arranged marriage. Clearly, it was a good match. Mary held her head high and didn't look down when spoken to as she used to do. Emma longed to feel the confidence she had once had and hold her head high again. But how could she ever get that back?

There would be no Silas for her. No man would want to swoop in and rescue her now.

Not that she wanted to be rescued. Not exactly. And Emma sensed that Mary hadn't been rescued, either. She seemed to have found someone who confirmed that she had been worth loving all along. Emma wanted a partner and friend, like Mary had found. She wanted to encourage a man while he encouraged her. She wanted that togetherness that can only come with mutual respect, trust, and, of course, love.

"Emma, it's so *gut* to see you," Mary said as she strode toward Emma. One thing had not changed; Mary's soft, warm smile was as genuine as ever.

"Hi, Mary." Emma looked down. She realized that she must look just as Mary used to—as if she knew she were worthless. Even so, she couldn't bring herself to raise her eyes. In the background, she could hear the murmur of women's voices as they bustled past one another in the small kitchen. They would all be staring at her, judging her. Emma had never heard of another woman in Bluebird Hills getting into the kind of trouble that she had. Mary had certainly never run around during *Rumspringa*. She had always been wholesome and good. Emma had never quite understood why Mary had always seemed so down on herself, when she had no reason to be. Not like Emma did.

Mary pulled Emma into a hug. Her arms were stronger, the embrace fiercer than Emma would have expected. "I'm so glad you're here," Mary said. She whispered into Emma's ear, "You're as *willkumm* here as anyone. Don't let anyone make you feel otherwise." Then she pulled back and added loud enough for the room to hear, "I've known Emma since she was just a little thing.

She hasn't been to Bluebird Hills to visit in a while, so let's make sure she feels *willkumm, ya*?" Mary turned her gaze on the women surrounding them. She gave them a no-nonsense look that Emma did not think Mary was capable of. There was a moment of awkward silence, before that familiar smile returned and the background buzz resumed.

"I was just about to make the biscuits," Mary said to Emma. "This was all unexpected, of course, so there isn't time to make bread that has to rise."

Emma nodded.

"Now, I remember that you make *abbeditlich* biscuits, ain't so?"

"Um, *vell*, I'm not sure how delicious they are…" Emma looked down at her hands as she twisted them together.

"I'd love for us to work together. Is that *oll recht*?"

Emma managed a small smile. "*Ya*. I'd like that." Emma knew that Mary was sparing her from having to interact with the other women. She understood that it was too overwhelming. "*Danki*, Mary."

Mary winked at Emma before turning to pull a sack of flour from the cabinet. They mixed the dough, rolled it out, and cut out the biscuits while Edna and a handful of other women chopped and stirred and baked. Viola sat on a stool, directing the activity. Every once in a while, she would tap her cane on the ground and bark a reminder about the best way to fry a chicken, or how much sugar to add to the tea.

After a while, Emma almost forgot the tension. She liked working in Mary's cozy little kitchen, with its light green cabinets and matching light green Formica countertops, even though the space was cramped and she bumped into the round dinette table a few times. The room had not been renovated since it had been built in the 1940s and Emma felt nostalgic as she slid the tray of biscuit dough into the gas-powered oven.

"Hey, we haven't met yet," a woman's voice said from behind Emma. She startled, straightened up fast, and spun around. A teenager smiled at her. She was a cheerful-looking girl with dark blond hair, big brown eyes, and a button nose. "I'm Mary's stepdaughter, Becky."

"Oh, hi. Nice to meet you."

Becky's eyes slid down, registered Emma's baby bump, and widened. She recovered quickly, but Emma still felt the sting of the shock. "You must be Emma?" Becky asked.

Emma cringed inside. Even strangers knew who she was. "*Ya.* I, uh, just moved in with Bishop Amos and Edna—my aunt and uncle." The familiar awkwardness rushed back. How

much to say? How much to explain? Becky
didn't look too interested in the gossip-worthy
event that had landed Emma in this situation.
But still...

"*Ach*, there you are." Mary rushed forward.
"*Danki* for running to the store for us, Becky."
She glanced at the clock on the wall. "Lunchtime
will be here before we know it. You got everything on the list?"

Becky nodded.

"Including the lemon juice for the lemon pies?"

"Yep."

Mary exhaled. "*Danki*. I don't know what
I would do without you, Becky." She took the
brown paper grocery bag. "Trying to feed all
these people and running out of sugar!" Mary
shook her head and laughed. "Whew. *Vell*, let's
get this done."

"It was no problem," Becky said, but her expression showed that she appreciated her step-
mother's praise.

Mary threw an arm around the girl's shoulder
and squeezed. "Can you start on the lemon pies?"

"Sure can."

Emma was relieved when Becky didn't ask
her any more questions. Instead, she told her
about a big volleyball tournament in Pinecraft,
Florida, and a boy named Noah who was courting her. Emma tried to smile and show her en-

thusiasm, but all she could think was that even sixteen-year-old girls had a chance for romance.

But Emma had thrown that chance away. She knew she would never get it back now.

Worse than hearing about Becky's courtship was having to go back outside, into the crowd, to serve lunch. Mary's house was too small to fit all the folding tables, so they set them up in the front yard, beneath the row of maple trees. Emma avoided looking over at the barn, but she could hear the tap of hammers and the whine of handsaws cutting through wood. She didn't want to feel the shame when the men looked back at her. Especially Benjamin. Her skin prickled as she set a big plastic jug of homemade lemonade onto one of the folding tables.

Emma tried to keep her eyes focused on the ground as she doubled back with the tray of biscuits. But she could not stop herself from peeking in Benjamin's direction. He stood in the grass alongside the barn wall with a hammer in one hand and a nail in the other. His brow crinkled in concentration as he swung the hammer down. He pulled his fingers back too quickly and the nail dropped to the ground instead of driving into the board. He grimaced and glanced around quickly. Emma knew he was checking to see if anyone had seen his mistake. She dropped her eyes fast, before he could catch her watching. Sweet Benjamin. He always tried so hard, but sometimes he just couldn't get things quite right. The other *youngies* used to make fun of him, but Emma had always stood up for him. She didn't care if he wasn't the best carpenter—or the best at anything, for that matter. She cared that he was thoughtful and kind and insightful. In fact, *not* being the best was probably what made him so kind. He knew what it was like to be looked down on.

Emma's heart swelled and she tamped the feeling down. How silly to think of Benjamin right now. They had been childhood friends, nothing more. And they were not even friends anymore. Sure, he had come to her rescue earlier, but that was just the kind of man he was. It didn't mean anything.

"Becky, go tell the men it's time to eat," Mary said as she set a stack of plates onto the table. Emma had not noticed that either of them were standing near her. Had she been that distracted by Benjamin? Emma shook her head, then straightened the pile of silverware. She needed something to do with her hands.

Becky jogged over to the barn and shouted, "Food's on the table!" There was a cheer from the men before they filed down the ladder like ants on their way to a picnic. Since Benjamin had been working from the ground, he just threw down his hammer and trotted over.

"Hey," he said with a friendly grin. "What have you made? Your cooking was always *gut*."

Emma laughed. "Don't lie, Benjamin Stoltzfus. You know I've never been a *gut* cook."

Benjamin just shrugged and smiled. "I like your cooking. Anyway, it's the thought that counts, ain't so?"

Emma couldn't help but return the smile. *"Ya,"* she said, and looked away as she felt the emotion swell within her. "It is."

The voices of hungry men overtook their quiet conversation as the workers trooped over and began grabbing plates from the stack. Emma stepped back and watched as they piled servings of fried chicken, green bean casserole, biscuits, and applesauce onto their plates. Benjamin nodded at her as he walked by with a very full plate, toward one of the tables.

But, before he could sit down, Miriam Stoltzfus stalked over and pulled him away from the crowd. Benjamin's face fell, then he glanced over at Emma with a strange expression that she couldn't quite decipher. Emma looked away fast, but Benjamin had already caught her staring. Her face heated and she knew that she was blushing. She tried to slip between Amos and a man she didn't recognize in order to hide behind the crowd.

Miriam's voice carried over the yard. She was too far away to make out the words, but the tone was sharp and guarded. Emma burned with the need to know exactly what Miriam was telling Benjamin. Was it about her? She snuck a quick peek from behind the crowd of men and saw that Miriam and Benjamin were both staring at her with frowns on their faces. Emma didn't like the look in Benjamin's eyes. Was it anger? Frustration? Could it be condemnation? Had he only been nice to her face, just to talk bad about her behind her back? That wasn't like him, but they had been apart for a long time. He might have changed. People did. She certainly had.

The thought lay heavy in her heart as she fell into line behind the women while they waited on the men to finish serving themselves. She had lost her appetite, but she would force the food down as she had been for the last eight months, for the baby's sake. That was all that mattered now. Her tiny precious baby.

It was just the two of them now.

Benjamin scowled at his sister.

"Benji, stop looking at me like that," Miriam said.

"Then stop talking to me like this."

Emma was standing across the lawn near the serving table, a few feet apart from the rest of the women as they waited in line to eat. Her face was flushed red and her eyes were on the ground. Benjamin felt a stab of frustration at his sister. Had Emma guessed that they were talking about her? Was that why she looked so lost and fragile right now? It wasn't right. Emma had always been boisterous and full of life. Where had that carefree girl gone?

"Keep your voice down and no one will know what we are discussing," Miriam shot back.

"I'm not the one being so obvious."

Miriam paused, took a deep breath, and exhaled. A muscle in her cheek jumped as she fought to keep her emotions in check. "I'm just worried, Benji. You can understand that, can't you?"

"You don't need to worry about me, Miriam."

Miriam raised her eyebrows.

"Stop giving me that look."

"Then stop making a public display of your feelings for Emma."

"A public display? What's the matter with you? We're friends! Can't friends say hello to one another? We've barely spoken in years."

"A lot has changed during those years, Benji."

"And a lot has stayed the same." He scowled at her. "I feel like I literally just had this conversation a few hours ago with Amanda."

"And you didn't listen. So now I have to get involved."

"You're my sister, not my mother. You'll never

be my mother. And besides, I'm a grown man, Miriam. How about you start recognizing that?"

Miriam flinched. Her voice lowered and Benjamin could hear a slight quaver in it. "I never tried to be our mother, Benji. I just want to..." She looked away. Her eyes still glittered with emotion, but her face had fallen. She looked smaller than she had a moment ago. She had a short, stout frame, but her demeanor usually made her seem bigger than she was. Benjamin sighed. Now he had managed to hurt two women in as many minutes.

"I'm sorry, Miriam. I didn't mean that." Miriam had always put the family first since their parents died. She had taken her younger siblings' burdens on her own shoulders and carried them all without complaint, even when it meant losing her chance at a family of her own. But it had hardened her, that was certain sure. She wasn't always easy to live with. Benjamin sifted through his thoughts and emotions, trying to put them all in order. And all the while, he could feel Emma's gaze burning into him. What was she thinking right now?

Miriam stood frozen for a moment. Then she forced a neutral expression onto her face and nodded. "It's *oll recht*. I know you didn't mean it the way it sounded."

Benjamin just stared back at her, trying to

come up with the right words. He had so much to say, but he didn't want to hurt her feelings again. Not after all she did for him. He knew that she meant well, no matter how infuriating she could be.

"I shouldn't have brought it up here." Miriam's face tightened. "I just wanted to warn you before it was too late. Once you cross a certain line, it's hard to go back again."

"Cross a line? You and Amanda act as if I'm proposing to her or something. I'm just being friendly. You should be friendly to her too. Have you thought about that?"

Miriam rubbed her temples, as if she had a headache. "*Ya.* I have. And I'm sorry for what Emma's going through. I really am. But she is not my concern. You are. I have to look out for you first, Benji. You are my responsibility, not her."

"Maybe I'm not your responsibility anymore, Miriam."

Miriam swallowed hard. She raised her chin slightly. "You'll always be my responsibility, Benji. I'm not your mother, but I love you like one. Please don't ever forget that. An older sister doesn't stop protecting her brother, no matter how old he gets."

Benjamin gave her a level stare. His heart thudded as he gathered the courage to say what he wanted to say to her. "Maybe I don't need protecting."

Miriam stared back for a long, hard moment. The pounding of his heart marked the seconds as they ticked by. Finally, Miriam dropped her gaze, shook her head, and sighed. "*Ach*, Benji. The fact that you don't see the danger means that you need protecting more than ever before." And then she turned on her heels and stalked away. She held her head high, but Benjamin could sense the pain he had caused in her. How could he ever be there for Emma *and* Miriam? They both meant the world to him. It was an impossible situation.

Benjamin turned his attention back to Emma. She looked so unapproachable and alone as she stood among a crowd of people, but separate from them. A breeze ruffled her apron and *kapp* strings. A wisp of honey-blond hair escaped her bun and the wind whipped it around her face, like a halo. Benjamin thought she looked like a painting. A beautiful, perfect painting. He wanted to rush to her, take her in his arms, and promise her that everything would be all right. He would make sure of it.

But instead, he looked away.

He had no idea what else to do.

Chapter Five

Benjamin didn't speak to Emma again at the work frolic. He focused on his work instead. But he couldn't help glancing over his shoulder every now and again to see if she were around. She never was. He imagined her hiding in the kitchen, scrubbing the dirty dishes in silence. He wondered how the other women were treating her. Mary and Becky would be welcoming, he was sure of that. But some of the others probably wouldn't be.

The ride home was strained and silent. Benjamin clenched the reins tight in his hands and kept his eyes on the road as Clyde plodded onward. Fluffy white clouds swept across the sky, blotting out the sun, then allowing the bright rays to break through again. Benjamin squinted against the glare as he hunched over the reins, his jaw set and his shoulders tight.

Leah sat on the bench seat beside him, looking like she wanted to ask him a question. But she never said anything. Instead, she turned her head away to watch the cornfields and pastures roll past the buggy. He heard a sigh from the seat behind him and knew exactly who it was. Only Miriam gave that long-suffering sigh. And only Miriam could make him feel guilty *and* full of righteous indignation at the same time.

When they finally wound up the gravel driveway and the buggy rocked to a stop, Benjamin could not leap out fast enough. He pushed open the barn door without looking back, then patted Clyde on the neck as his sisters climbed down from their seats. "How about some oats, *ya*?" The horse whinnied and nudged Benjamin's chest with his muzzle. He kept his focus on the horse, but he could hear his sisters' footsteps moving away, along with the murmur of their conversation.

Clyde plodded into the barn alongside Benjamin without complaint. He was a good horse, too old and tired to ever give Benjamin any trouble. He gave the horse another pat as the buggy wheels whined against the concrete floor. Clyde stopped exactly where he always did and swung his head around to stare at Benjamin with his wet, black eyes. "You look as worn out from the day as I do," Benjamin murmured as he began to unbuckle the harness. "It's been a lot, ain't so?"

Benjamin heard someone enter the barn and he braced himself. When he looked up, Leah was standing beside him with crossed arms. Her skin was fairer than her siblings, her hair a lighter brown, and she had a light spray of freckles that always made her look cute instead of annoyed. But whenever Benjamin told her this, it always made her even more annoyed. "I knew something was bothering you," she said.

"Hey, Leah."

"So what's wrong?"

"*Ach*, that was a conversation between Clyde and me. You weren't supposed to hear."

Leah laughed. Then her expression turned serious. "I don't need to hear you venting to the horse to know something is bothering you."

Benjamin sighed. The metal buckles rattled as he unhitched the harness.

"We don't keep things from each other."

"*Ya*, I know." Benjamin shrugged. "I just don't know what to say."

"You can start with what you're feeling."

"I don't know what I'm feeling." His fingers tightened around the leather harness, then he spun around. "Miriam and Amanda won't leave it alone."

"Leave what alone?"

He looked down and kicked a clod of dirt that Clyde had tracked inside. "Emma."

"Right. Of course." Leah shifted her weight from one foot to the other.

"So, you agree with them?"

"*Nee.* That's not what I meant. I meant of course they're going to worry about it."

"Come on, Leah. Worry about what, exactly?"

Leah let out a breath through pursed lips.

"It sounds like you agree with them."

"I haven't said anything about it yet."

"And that says it all."

"Look, whatever you're feeling toward them is between them and you. Please don't get defensive with me. I'm here to help. Or try to, at least."

Benjamin grunted. "You're right. I'm sorry." He slid the bit from Clyde's mouth. The horse snorted and shook his head. "So what *do* you think about Emma being back?"

Leah frowned. "I think it's got to be really hard on her to be in the situation she's in. I think we should do whatever we can to make things easier for her."

Benjamin's eyes flashed. "Exactly!"

Leah put a hand on his arm. "But it isn't that simple."

"Some things don't have to be as complicated as you all want to make them. I know you look at me and think that just because I'm clumsy, or can't figure out math, or can't remember to shut the gate, that I don't catch on to things. *Vell,* I do. I'm not slow, Leah." Benjamin tapped his temple. "Not in here, anyway. I just can't get it across to people like I want to."

"I know, Benji."

He sighed. "I know you do, Leah. I'm sorry I got a little heated there. It's just frustrating. Somehow, I always end up looking like I don't know what I'm doing or talking about."

"We know you're smart, Benji."

Emotion flared behind Benjamin's eyes. "*You* do, but does the rest of the family?"

"Yes, they just don't always know how to handle it."

Benjamin unlatched Clyde's stall. He didn't need any encouragement, but plodded inside on his own, tail swishing, head down. "There isn't anything to handle. They need to stop treating me like I'm a child. We're the same age, but they treat you like you're one of them."

Leah didn't respond. She just leaned her elbows over the stall wall and watched Clyde bury his muzzle in the feed trough. After a minute, she pushed away from the wall. "You're right. They do treat us differently."

"Because I'm different. You don't struggle to do things that come easily for everyone else."

"We're all different, in our own ways."

"*Vell*, some ways are more obvious and more challenging than others."

"*Ya*, that's true. And it's not fair. It just isn't

and it never will be. Because life isn't fair." Leah studied Benjamin's expression for a moment. "But the truth is, people like you because you're not like everyone else. *I* like you because of that." She raised her eyebrows knowingly. "Emma always liked you because of that."

Benjamin gave a nervous laugh. "So do you think she still likes me?"

Leah's expression shifted. "*Ach*, Benji. I don't know."

Benjamin's stomach dropped. "Never mind. I shouldn't have asked."

"She ought to still like you," Leah said quickly. She paused and licked her lips. "But things have changed… She may not be in a good place emotionally right now when it comes to that kind of thing. She might need some time."

"*Ya*, she might. Or she might need a friend."

"*Ya*, she might." Leah smiled. "And the only way you'll find out is if you ask her."

After lunch the next day, Emma pinned on a work kerchief over her bun, slipped on her green garden gloves, and headed outside. While Edna and Amos took care of some shopping in town, she wanted to surprise them by weeding the kitchen garden and getting some planting done. She tried to be as useful as she could, but usually she just felt like she was in the way. Edna had run a well-oiled household for years and Emma couldn't quite figure out where to slide in and help. Especially since she couldn't carry anything heavy and was completely drained most of the time. And once the baby came, she would be even more of a bother.

No, she wouldn't think about that.

Edna and Amos said that every baby is a blessing and that they were happy for them both to stay as long as Emma wanted to be there. But Emma was afraid that they would grow weary of the burden. Besides, her family expected her to return to Holmes County eventually. But how could she face going home again, without a father for her child? She pushed the worry away and strode through the grassy lawn, to the side of the farmhouse. The autumn sky was bright blue and cloudless, as if the world were a bright, happy place without any troubles.

Emma headed for the zucchini, but she couldn't stop and focus on weeding the long rows of vegetables. Instead, she thought about the place where she and Benjamin used to escape to when they were upset, back when they were children. Emma didn't hesitate. She peeled off her gloves and dropped them beside a cabbage without slowing her pace. She would come back and weed the garden later. Right now, she was going to the spot where she had always felt the safest.

Emma was out of breath when she reached the split rail fence that separated the Yoder farm from Stoneybrook Farm. She followed it until she passed beneath the old, towering oak tree, its golden yellow leaves fluttering in the breeze, then picked her way down a sharp embankment and up another hill.

She stopped at the crest of the hill. There, at the bottom of the long, sloped incline lay a carpet of yellow-and-brown sunflowers. Each flower swayed gently on a tall, green stalk, its face turned toward the sun to soak up the rays. Beyond the field of flowers, a lake shimmered in the afternoon light and reflected the yellow petals on the surface of the water. Emma stood and stared for a moment, taking in the beauty as her body remembered the peace she had always felt in this place.

Soon, she was sweeping down the hill, without even realizing it. Her feet flew as fast as they could with the extra passenger on board, the wind fluttering her work kerchief and whipping the skirt of her dress behind her. She had not felt that free in a very long time. This was home, truly home, where she belonged.

If only Benjamin was here. He was the one thing missing. They used to spend hours wandering the long rows of flowers, lying beneath their shade and chatting, then running to the lake and leaping in when the summer heat grew too fierce. Afterward, they would stretch out on the bank until their clothes dried in the sun. They had told each other their troubles, their hopes and dreams. Here, in the sunflower field, their secrets were safe.

And then they grew up.

Emma slowed down before she reached the edge of the field and eased between the tall rows of flowers. The familiar, earthy scent met her along with the dappled shadows cast by the stalks and petals. She shouldn't think about Benjamin being here. That was a child's thought. Adults didn't laugh and cry together in a field of flowers. It was time to move on.

"Hey, that's not..." Benjamin's voice called out from behind a row of flowers.

Emma couldn't see him but she would know that voice anywhere.

"Emma, is that you?"

"Benjamin!" Emma could not stop the grin from overtaking her face. "I was just thinking about you!" Oh no. That had not come out quite right. Benjamin was a friend—a dear wonderful friend. But he was only a friend. "I mean, coming here reminded me of you. You know, because we used to spend so much time here together." She hoped that explanation would clear up any misunderstanding. It wasn't that she didn't think

Benjamin would make a wonderful husband and father—he certainly would—but she had never thought of him that way before.

The memory of him striding through the crowd at the work frolic popped into her mind. He had been so protective. His defense of her had stirred something in her heart that made her feel strange. She couldn't think of Benjamin that way, could she?

No, she could not.

And anyway, it was best that she didn't let herself go there. He could never be interested in her. Not now.

There was a rustling in the stalks. "Where are you?"

"I'm here!" Emma shouted.

More rustling. The stalks in front of her swayed, the dirt crunched, and Benjamin appeared. She smiled at him as he finished making his way toward her, gently picking past the flowers to keep from damaging them.

"I didn't expect to see you here," he said.

"Nee, vell..." She shrugged. "I guess I just needed to come here."

Benjamin puffed out his cheeks and exhaled. "Yeah. Me too." He ran his fingers through his tousled brown hair.

Emma wondered where his straw hat was. She

cocked her head as she studied him. "You *oll recht*?"

He gave a nervous chuckle. "*Ach*, I'm fine."

"I know you, Benjamin Stoltzfus, and I know when something's wrong."

Benjamin shrugged and flashed a sheepish smile. "Never could hide anything from you, Emma."

"*Vell*, don't try and start now. Tell me what's wrong."

"Uh, I feel like I should be asking you that, I mean—" Benjamin squeezed his eyes shut. He shook his head. "I didn't mean… Look, I just want you to know that you can talk to me too. You've got bigger problems than I do." Bright red splotches bloomed across his cheeks and overtook the skin on his neck. "I'm sorry, I didn't mean to suggest, to bring up…" He covered his face with a tan, calloused hand. "I'm no good at this. You know that. I hope you still know what I mean, even when I say the wrong thing."

"It's *oll recht*, Benjamin. I know."

He dropped his hand and forced himself to make eye contact with her, even though his face was still bright red. "Um, so…do you want to talk about…you know…"

"*Nee*." Emma said the word so fast that Benjamin flinched. He recovered quickly and gave her a little grin. "Then I guess I'll talk."

Emma covered her embarrassment with a playful grin. "You better." Her problem was so shameful that Benjamin couldn't even speak of it outright. She wondered what he would think if she told him all that had happened over the last year. Well, she would never find out because she would never let him know. She wanted him to remember her as the girl she had been, not the woman that everyone saw her as now.

"I guess you don't want to sit in the dirt, like we used to," Benjamin said.

"I haven't changed *that* much." Emma nudged him in the ribs with an elbow. "Besides, I'm wearing my work dress. I don't mind getting it dirty." She began to ease herself onto the ground. Benjamin shot forward, took her arm, and helped lower her down. *"Danki."* Her eyes locked onto his as she said the words and they lingered there a beat longer than she meant them to. When had his hands become so big? When had he become strong enough to bear her weight without any effort? A flicker of emotion shimmered through her. She didn't like the way that emotion drew her toward him and she shoved it away. "So." She stretched her legs out in front of her, straightened the skirt of her dress, and leaned back on the palms of her hands. "What's wrong?"

"Oh, right. I almost forgot." He cleared his

throat. "I, uh, *vell*, where do I begin?" He laughed and picked up a yellow oak leaf that had blown into the sunflower field.

"Wherever you want to."

Emma could sense the thoughts moving through his mind as his expression shifted. She suspected that he was sifting through what was okay to say and what was not.

"It's about my *schweschdre*."

Emma nodded. She wasn't surprised. Benjamin's sisters loved him, that was undeniable. But she had seen the older three suffocate him with that love.

"They worry about me."

"*Ya*, I know they do."

Benjamin twirled the oak leaf between his fingers. "I, uh, just want them to see that I'm capable of a lot more than they think I am." His eyes were on the yellow leaf. "And they said…" He shook his head and Emma sensed that he was holding back a lot of the story. Was it to spare her? What were they all saying about her? Well, she could certainly imagine. "They say too much sometimes. And it isn't so easy to shut them down."

"I can understand that." His sisters had always intimidated her. They were a united front, full of grit and determination. Miriam especially. Emma had rarely seen the woman smile. And one sharp look from Miriam used to scare her more than any other grown-up. Looking back, that seemed silly, since Miriam must have still been in her late teens back then. But she had always loomed larger than the older adults. Emma figured Miriam had to be that way in order to keep all the other siblings in line, especially since her stature was small and unintimidating.

Benjamin let go of the oak leaf and it fell to the ground. "I guess that's it."

Emma knew that wasn't all of it. But she wasn't going to press him, especially when it would probably end in her humiliation. She could not forget his sisters' expressions when they had looked at her at the work frolic. "I know it's not so easy to push back against them. You're a peacemaker and I like that about you—"

"You do?" Benjamin interrupted as his face lit up in a big goofy grin.

Emma gave his shoulder a playful nudge. "Men ought to focus on that more, if you ask me."

"You don't think it makes me weak? Most men, *vell*, you know, they don't want to seem like pushovers."

"You're not a pushover. You're a peacemaker. There's a difference. I saw how you stood up and defended me yesterday and I appreciated it." Emma stopped herself. "I just mean…" She didn't know how to explain how she felt about Benjamin, exactly. "You understand what I'm trying to say?"

"I think so."

"*Oll recht*, then, that's settled."

Benjamin chuckled. "*Oll recht*, then."

"So, what do you think you can do about this problem with your *schweschdre* that won't cause too much division?"

"I'd like to do more on the farm, you know, have my own part of it. I feel like I'm always trying to catch up to whatever they're doing. If I could just do my own thing, then I could…" His voice trailed off.

"You don't have to prove anything to them, Benji."

"*Ya*, I do."

Emma didn't respond right away. She just nodded to let Benjamin know she understood. "So, what would you like to do on the farm, if you could do anything?"

Benjamin shrugged, but Emma could see the idea flicker across his face.

"Just tell me."

"*Ach*, it's *lecherich*."

"I've never thought any of your ideas are ridiculous." Emma grinned at him. "A little out of the box, maybe. But never ridiculous."

Benjamin gave a shy shrug. "I'd like to launch

a soap-making business. I hear *Englischers* love goat milk soap." His voice sped up and his gestures became more animated as he continued. "I've been doing the research. I know it could sell well. Maybe I could help the farm. We barely scrape by sometimes, you know. I could open up a stall at the farmers market in town. And I could sell directly from our farm, too. I could put out a sign and the *Englisch* tourists would see it and drive up to the house. The Glicks sell their homemade root beer right out of their kitchen, ain't so? It gives them a decent side income."

"You should go for it."

"Do you really mean that?"

"Of course I do."

"*Ach*, I don't know." He scratched his head, leaving his hair more tousled than it already was. "The business side of things might not work out. I'm not so *gut* at arithmetic and all that."

"It'll work out. At least think about it. You've got a *gut* idea."

"You really think so?"

"*Ya*. I really do."

Chapter Six

Benjamin had an extra spring in his step as he walked back to his house. He whistled as he went and stopped to appreciate how fast a squirrel could scramble up a tree trunk, then soar from one branch to another. The leaves of the old oak shook from the animal's sudden weight. He smiled as he gazed upward into the golden, sun-drenched foliage, before turning his attention down the hill, to where Emma stood in Edna's kitchen garden. She looked up as she pulled on a set of green garden gloves. Benjamin grinned when their eyes met, threw up a hand in an enthusiastic wave, then turned and trotted home.

Emma had given him the confidence that he needed. He wished that he could have told her everything, but that would have hurt her. And, he would have had to admit how strong his feelings were for her. No, it was best that he never told her that. And not just because it would end in his humiliation. She deserved a friend who was there for her simply because of who she was, not because he secretly longed for a relationship. He would not pursue anything more than friendship with her.

It was enough that she had called him Benji, his old childhood nickname. No one but his sisters ever called him that—and Emma, back when they had been close. It made him feel like the closeness between them was reforming. Maybe they really would be friends forever, even if it didn't look the same way it had as when they were children. It couldn't, of course. But he would accept whatever form their friendship took now. She was worth it. She was the best friend he had ever had.

And now, after their conversation, he felt like he wasn't alone in the battle of wills between him and his sisters anymore. He decided he wouldn't be stopped, not this time. He would go right up to them and ask—no, tell—them what he was going to do. He jogged across the farmyard, thudded up the porch steps, flung open the farmhouse door, and burst inside. "Hey, everyone! I've got an idea. Guess what I'm going to do?"

He flew down the hall and tumbled into the kitchen, slid on a slick patch of linoleum, and skidded to a stop. Viola Esch sat at the big wooden table, a mug in her hands. Her eyebrows shot up. "What are you going to do, young man?"

"Oh." He glanced at Miriam, who stood at the counter, pouring coffee, then to Amanda, who was slicing a shoofly pie. "I didn't realize we had company."

Naomi strode past the open door and pivoted to a stop. "There you are, Benji. It's almost time for the evening milking."

"*Ya*. I know. I'm here in time for it."

Naomi frowned. "Barely. I was just headed out to do all of it, since you weren't here."

"I'm here for it."

"*Vell*, now you are."

Viola tapped her cane on the floor. "First, he's going to tell me about this big idea of his."

Miriam held out the mug of coffee she had just poured and nodded toward Naomi. "We've got a few minutes before the milking has to get done. *Kumme* visit with Viola a minute. You can fill in for me. I need to—"

Naomi shot Miriam a look. "*Ach*, *nee*, I'd love to, but I've still got the washing to take off the line."

Benjamin stifled a smile. Miriam always tried to get out of Viola's visits. She never had the patience to sit through the lectures. Neither did Naomi. Benjamin didn't mind, though. Viola made him laugh and he knew that she meant well, even when she meddled.

"All of you *kumme* sit," Viola said. "I'm here

for a visit, and I mean to have one. Now, let's hear your news, Benjamin." She adjusted her glasses and leaned toward him. She was a thin woman, all knobby knees and elbows. And with her skinny, wrinkled neck jutted out like that, she reminded him of a turtle.

Benjamin would rather not spill his idea to Viola, because it meant the entire church district would know by the end of the week. But then again, that might keep his sisters from shutting him down. Especially if he could get Viola on his side. She had a special talent for getting her way. Besides, it was fun to watch his sisters squirm while having to sit still and listen. It was the only time Miriam lost control in her own house. Funny how powerful a little old woman could be.

Benjamin grinned. "Sounds *gut*. I'll just get a big slice of pie first." Amanda rolled her eyes as she passed him a plate. He just winked back at her. A minute later they were all gathered around the table with steaming mugs of coffee and fresh shoofly pie. Benjamin couldn't resist shoving a sticky, syrupy bite into his mouth before getting started. He chewed fast, swallowed hard, and wiped his mouth with his napkin. "I'm starting a goat milk soap business."

Miriam frowned. "We haven't talked about this."

"*Nee, vell*, I'm doing it on my own…so…" He shrugged and looked down at his plate.

"Do you have a business plan?" Amanda asked.

Viola waved her hand. "He doesn't need a business plan. It's a *gut* idea. He makes the soap, he sells it. What's there to plan?"

The sisters all glanced at one another. "I mean, *vell*…" Naomi cleared her throat. "You're right, it's a *gut* idea. But it might not be so simple to get off the ground. There's the overhead, the cost of production, how much milk there is to spare for this new stream of business—"

"We have enough," Benjamin interrupted. "Our orders have been a little down lately. You know that. That's what gave me the idea. We've been trying to drink the extra ourselves, or give it away so it doesn't go to waste, ain't so?"

Naomi frowned. "*Ya*, that's true. There's probably enough to spare. But we should run the numbers first."

Benjamin shrugged. "Okay, so I'll run the numbers."

Miriam and Amanda exchanged a quick look. Miriam's brow crinkled. Benjamin hated that look. It was full of sympathy, but it always meant that she was going to shut him down because she didn't think he was capable. The worst thing was, when it came to figuring sums, she was right.

"Maybe running the numbers yourself isn't the best idea," Miriam said quietly. She shook her head. "We can talk about that later."

Viola waved her hand in a dismissive gesture. "*Nee*, let's talk about it now, while I'm here to solve the problem."

"*Danki*, Viola," Amanda said. "But I don't think there's a problem to solve. We'll handle it."

"You're right." Viola raised her chin. "There isn't a problem, because I've already solved it."

Miriam squeezed the bridge of her nose with her fingers.

Naomi shifted in her seat.

Amanda sighed.

Viola just smiled. "I'm headed over to pay a visit to the bishop after this. I'll make sure he sends Emma over to help. Three or four afternoons a week should do it. She needs to stay busy and earn some extra money, ain't so? It'll be *gut* for her. She'll be able to handle all the math and whatever else Benjamin can't do."

Benjamin frowned at such a direct statement about his disability, but he didn't let it bother him too much. Good old Viola had come through for him. Once she got an idea in her head, no one could stop her. Not even Miriam.

"*Ach, nee.*" Miriam stiffened. Suddenly, her spine was as straight as a board. "That won't be necessary. We'll handle it all—"

"Nonsense." Viola made a shooing motion with her hand, then began to push herself up with her cane. Benjamin jumped up and helped lift her from her seat. She gave him a nod. "*Danki*, young man. I'm going to get over there now. This is such a *gut* idea that I'm not going to wait. We're going to get Emma over here as soon as possible."

Naomi let out a sharp exhale.

Amanda looked panicked.

"I can see you all agree," Viola said as she hobbled toward the doorway.

"*Nee*, actually, it's better not to involve Emma in this," Miriam said.

Viola's cane stopped tapping across the floor. She froze and turned around slowly. "And why not, exactly?"

"Because, *vell*, you know, it just isn't..." Miriam looked flustered as she glanced at Amanda and Naomi for support. Miriam never looked flustered. And she was never at a loss for words.

Viola raised an eyebrow. "It just isn't *what*, dear?"

Miriam's lips formed a tight line.

"*Gut*. That's what I thought. I knew an up-standing Amish sister like you would never try to keep another Amish sister from being a part of the community."

"Nee," Miriam answered through gritted teeth. "Of course not."

Viola grinned. *"Vell,* glad that's settled, then." And she was out the door before anyone else could think of what to say. They heard her cane tapping down the long hallway. The front door opened and closed, leaving them in silence.

And still, no one said a word.

Emma could not believe what she was hearing. "I'm not sure I understand," she said to Amos and Edna as she set the basket of fresh-picked zucchini onto the kitchen table. "Can you repeat that?"

Amos glanced at Edna and she nodded reassuringly. "We think it's a *gut* idea for you to help Benjamin launch a goat milk soap side business," he said. "You can start tomorrow."

Emma tried to process the information. "Benjamin wants me to help? He asked for me? Because I was just talking to him about this earlier today and he didn't say anything about wanting me to be involved."

"Ach, vell..." Amos stroked his long white beard. "That doesn't mean he doesn't want you there...necessarily."

"Just because he didn't mention that he wanted your help doesn't mean that he doesn't want it," Edna jumped in.

"But if he didn't ask for my help…" Emma folded her arms across her chest. "What gave you the idea? How did you even know about it? I know news travels fast on the Amish telegraph, but this is spreading as fast at the *Englisch* internet." Emma stopped short. She suddenly realized what was happening. "Was that Viola who just paid a visit?" Emma had heard a buggy pull up to the front of the farmhouse and had purposely stayed hidden in the kitchen garden. She was still trying to avoid as many people as she could. She had only come back inside once she heard the familiar crunch of gravel beneath buggy wheels and the clip-clop of hooves moving away, toward the highway at the bottom of the long driveway.

Amos cleared his throat. "Uh, *ya.* That was Viola. She thinks it's a *gut* idea. Benjamin needs help with the business side of things and you need, *vell*…" He cleared his throat again. "Some extra money wouldn't hurt…" Amos raised his hands, palms up. "I know Viola can have some *lecherich* ideas, but I agree with this one. You need to get out more. You need a friend."

Emma looked away. The familiar sting of shame pricked her cheeks. "I haven't forgotten what Viola said during her last visit. She's trying to make a match between Benjamin and me."

An awkward silence filled the room. "Would

that be such a bad thing?" Edna asked gently. "He's a *gut* man and you've always liked one another."

"As friends."

"Friendship is the best foundation for a *gut* marriage."

Emma shook her head. "I don't think you understand. The problem isn't that I don't want to spend time with him. It's that he may not want me there. And I'm pretty sure his *schweschdre* don't. This could go very badly. Can't you see that?"

"Viola said that he and his *schweschdre* all agreed to it," Amos said.

Emma squeezed her eyes shut. "Agreed to it? Or got backed into a corner by Viola?"

Silence.

Emma's eyes flew open. She looked directly at Edna. "It's better for me to stay here."

"You can't hide away forever," Edna said. "And going to the work frolic wasn't so bad, was it?"

"I've known the Stoltzfus sisters since they were born," Amos chimed in. "They've had to be tough in order to run that farm on their own, especially Miriam. She carries a lot on her shoulders. She was still a *youngie* when all that responsibility landed on her. It's hardened her, but I believe her heart is still soft. Maybe she will surprise you."

"And maybe she won't," Emma said. "I'm sorry. I don't mean to argue with you. I'm just afraid of going over to the farm tomorrow and finding out that they don't want me there."

Amos's eyes looked sad. He nodded. "You're right. If we're honest with ourselves, we have to recognize that could happen. I'm not going to pressure you into it. It's your decision. We'll support you either way. Just promise me that you'll think about it. Spending time with Benjamin might end up being a very *gut* thing."

Or it might not, Emma thought. But she did not say it out loud. She had already said too much. "I don't want to go against what you think is best, but…"

"It's *oll recht*," Amos said. "We're not going to push you into a match. We're here to support you."

"Do you really mean that?" Emma asked in a quiet voice.

"Of course we do."

In the midst of everything, Emma felt a reassuring warmth deep inside. Her aunt and uncle would be here for her, no matter what. She might not have a father for this baby, but she would never be without family. And knowing that would help give her the strength to keep going, even if everyone else around her turned their backs.

* * *

Emma tossed and turned all night. She could not decide what to do. She listened to the creak of the wooden floorboards in the attic above her and the sigh of the wind as it passed through the orchard and shook the branches. The pillow felt lumpy no matter how many times she punched it down. She was too hot under the quilt, then too cold without it. And by morning, she still had not made a decision.

The time came when Benjamin would be expecting her to show up at his doorstep. Emma wanted to go and she did not want to go. In the end, she found herself putting on her black athletic shoes and tying the laces, even though she had not decided yet. Her body just took over, went through the motions of getting ready, and next thing she knew, she was marching up the hill, through the gate, and into the Stoltzfus farmyard. Their guard dog, Ollie, loped over to her, sniffed her hand, and allowed her to pass by without barking. He still remembered her. The realization tugged at her heart. Everything felt so familiar, so right, even though it had been a few years since she had been here. Just as they always had, the goats bleated in the distance and the diesel-powered machinery hummed quietly in the production building. The big, weathered farmhouse with the double porch and tin roof looked the same. Her baby kicked and Emma's hand moved to her belly. Well, not everything was just as it was.

Emma raised her chin, set her shoulders, and strode up the front porch steps. The old boards creaked beneath her weight. She had not made it to the door before Benjamin threw open the screen and popped outside, a big grin on his face. "Hey, there you are. I thought you might not..."

Emma smiled. "Of course I was going to come." And she realized that she meant it. "I didn't mean to be late."

"Oh, are you late?" Benjamin rubbed the back of his neck. "I, uh, wasn't really paying attention."

Dishes clattered from inside the farmhouse, followed by a thud and the sound of pouring water.

"Let's go out to the barn, *oll recht*? I've got a place for us to work there." Benjamin led them back down the porch steps and across the farmyard to a room in the corner of the barn. The walls were unpainted and weathered, and a few of the wooden boards had cracks between them that allowed beams of light to filter through. Dust motes floated in the air, highlighted by the afternoon sun. Benjamin hurried to pull a battered wooden chair up to a folding table. "Here, have a seat." He stepped back and looked around. "I know it isn't much, but…" He shrugged. "We'll make something of it, ain't so?"

"For certain sure." Their eyes met and a flare of excitement sparked inside Emma's chest. It was easy to ignore the dirt floor, the stacks of broken crates, the feed bags in the corner, and the damp smell of old wood when she saw Benjamin's enthusiasm. "It's rustic."

"I've been working most of the day to clean it up. This is as *gut* as it's going to get."

"It's plenty *gut*." Emma took a deep breath and sank into the chair. "Now, where should we start?"

She spent the afternoon poring over the numbers, figuring out exactly how much the farm could spare on the start-up costs and how much profit it would take to make the project viable. They made a budget and a shopping list, then Emma leaned back in her chair, stretched her back, and sighed. "I think we've got the basics taken care of."

"Then it's time for some lemonade and cake, ain't so? I think you've earned it."

Emma laughed. "You don't have to convince me." She was always hungry these days.

"You are eating for two." Benjamin flinched as soon as he said the words. Red splotches appeared on his face and he looked away. "I mean, um…" He cleared his throat and stood up. "Let's go get that cake."

Emma didn't know what to say. Benjamin clearly thought that he had crossed a line by acknowledging the obvious. But even if he didn't say anything, they both knew there was a baby coming soon. A baby who would not have a father. Emma's hands shook as she organized and stacked the papers. Was he so ashamed of her that he couldn't admit the truth? What would happen after the baby was born? Would he still go on pretending that she wasn't an unwed mother? The thought was ludicrous. Of all the people who Emma had hoped could face the truth about her, it was Benjamin.

But no, he could not face it. Or he did not want to. She wasn't even sure that she could blame him. She felt she deserved being an object of disapproval, a lesson of what *not* to do. She was no longer a person. She was an example.

Benjamin barely spoke as they filed out of the barn and into the bright sunlight. He wasn't smiling as they crossed the farmyard and skirted around a wheelbarrow. The kitchen windows of the farmhouse were open and the clang of pots and pans and the low murmur of women's voices drifted out over the grass and mud. Emma stiffened. Her footsteps slowed. She could not go in there and face the Stoltzfus sisters. Benjamin kept going a few paces before he noticed that she was no longer behind him. He turned around and an expression flickered over his face that she couldn't decipher.

"You, uh, changed your mind?" He nodded at the farmhouse. "If you want to just sit down on the porch, I'll bring the cake and lemonade out to you."

Was he trying to spare her from seeing his sisters? If that were the case, then he knew that they didn't want her there. Emma did not want to be anywhere that she wasn't wanted. She didn't want to have to sit on the porch because it was too shameful to invite her inside the house. And maybe Benjamin didn't want her coming inside, either. He had just pointed out her condition. Perhaps he had thought about it and decided that his sisters had a point. After all, he had choked up as soon as he acknowledged the pregnancy.

"Nee." Emma shook her head. "I just remembered that I have to help Edna with some extra chores today. I need to get on back. I'll, uh, see you tomorrow."

Benjamin's brows knitted together. "So, you're coming back?"

Emma could not read his tone of voice. She wasn't sure if he were asking because he wanted her to return—or because he didn't.

"Um, sure. I mean, that's the plan, right?"

she managed to ask before taking off across the farmyard. She did not slow down until she was too far away for Benjamin to make out the tears in her eyes.

Benjamin was baffled. He knew he had messed up, but he wasn't sure exactly how. Well, obviously he should not have mentioned the baby. *Eating for two.* He could not stop ruminating over the mistake he had made. While fetching a load of firewood, doing the milking, or mucking out the goat shed—*eating for two* kept repeating in his mind over and over. That was what had started the problem. He had offended her by bringing up her condition. Of course he had. It wasn't any of his business and he never should have pointed it out. He had forgotten, in that moment, to be careful. He had felt so close to her, as if they were truly friends again. And then he had gone and said something that made her feel ashamed. He should have fixed it, right then and there, but he had been afraid that he would just make it worse. He had a track record of doing that.

And as if that weren't bad enough, his sisters had all been in the kitchen. He had cleared out the tack room in the barn specifically so that he and Emma could avoid them. He had expected his sisters to be in the production building or he never would have suggested that Emma come to the house. His sisters might mean well, but the pain they caused would hurt Emma just as much as if their intentions were bad.

It didn't matter, in the end. Emma didn't want to stay and visit. She lit out of there as fast as she could. Did she think that he judged her as his sisters did? If so, what could he do about it? If he said anything, she might feel pressured to talk about it. He might cause her more shame. Better to leave it be and let her bring it up if she wanted to. That seemed like the most respectful thing to do.

But the tightness in his chest warned him that no matter what he did, this was not going to turn out well.

Chapter Seven

As soon as Emma got home, Edna insisted on taking her out to buy baby supplies. "And something nice for you too," she added.

Emma tried to refuse, but she couldn't convince Edna to cancel the outing.

"Nonsense," was all that Edna said in response. "Of course we're going shopping. Oh, and Sadie Kauffman—Sadie Lapp, back when you knew her—has already planned on joining us. You remember her, don't you? She's expecting a *boppli* too. Have you heard?"

Emma cringed inside. She knew that Sadie was happily married after a nannying job had led to an unexpected, fairy-tale romance. Sadie was cheerful, wholesome, and married. Everything that Emma was not.

Edna's face fell. "I'm sorry. I should have run that by you first… I just thought…"

"That I would say no?"

Edna gave a sheepish grin that showed she had been caught. *"Ya."* The smile faded quickly. "I just want you to find your way. Sadie's close to your age. I thought you could be friends."

Emma looked down. "That's not up to me."

Edna put a hand over Emma's. "If you don't give her a chance, how will you know?"

Emma took a deep breath and exhaled. "*Oll recht*. Let's go."

Sadie's buggy was already parked in the lot beside Beiler's Quilt and Fabric Shop when they arrived. She climbed down from the driver's seat looking as wholesome and cheerful as ever. Blond hair peeked out from beneath her *kapp*, her blue eyes sparkled, and her cheeks looked rosy. She landed on the pavement harder than she had meant to, laughed at herself, and put a hand to her belly. "I forget how heavy I am now."

Emma braced herself and stepped down from the Yoder buggy. "Hi, Sadie." She looked down and adjusted her apron.

"Hey, Emma." Sadie hurried over and pulled her into a big hug. "It's been too long. I'm so glad to see you again. And we're going to have fun getting *boppli* stuff together, ain't so?"

Emma was startled by the enthusiasm before she remembered how warm and welcoming Sadie had always been. That was just the kind of person she was. Emma began to feel a little less self-conscious. "*Ya*. I'm glad you could *kumme*."

Sadie linked arms with Emma and steered

them both toward the door of the fabric shop. Edna followed behind looking pleased and not at all surprised.

Betty Beiler was stacking quilt squares on a shelf when they strolled in. She looked up and her face froze when she saw Emma. Betty recovered quickly, but Emma had not missed the look. "What can I help you with today?" she asked.

"I didn't buy enough fabric to make everything we need for the *boppli* the last time I was here," Edna said. "And we're going to need fabric for a bigger maternity dress. We can't let this one out anymore."

Emma turned to a bolt of blue fabric across the aisle. She had to look at something, do something with her hands, anything to distract her from the fact that they were discussing her situation so openly, for the entire store to hear. Of course, everyone could see that she was expecting a *boppli*—and getting bigger every day—but she didn't want it acknowledged. She had hoped and prayed that she would be one of those women who carried small, so it wouldn't be so obvious. Instead, her stomach poked out so far that strangers had begun to ask her if she was having twins. She wasn't.

Emma ran her fingers down the blue cotton blend and tried to ignore what Emma and Betty were saying.

"Emma?"

Emma looked up to see Mary Hochstetler standing in front of her with an employee name tag pinned to her pink cape dress. "Oh. Hi, Mary. I heard you weren't working here anymore."

"*Vell*, business got pretty bad after the Sew-N-Save opened up across town, but our customers have been coming back to us now. I just come in every now and then, when Betty needs me. It's a *gut* arrangement. I always loved working here and it's nice to get out of the house sometimes. But I still have plenty of time to be with the *kinner* and work with Silas at our harness business."

Emma felt that familiar pang at the mention of family. She thought how wonderful it would be to work with her husband, side by side. She couldn't imagine Benjamin having a harness business, but soap making— Emma cut the thought short. What on earth had come over her? Why had Benjamin popped into her mind? She certainly was not going to ride off into the sunset with him and his soap-making business.

"I'm so happy to hear that, Mary." And she was. Truly. Even though it hurt that she didn't have what Mary had.

Mary hesitated. Emma could see that she was debating whether or not to say something. Mary shifted closer and lowered her voice. "You know, my life didn't work out the way I wanted for a long time. I had given up on ever getting married. But *Gott*, he knew the plans he had for me."

"Oh." It was the only word that Emma could get out. Was she that transparent? Mary's words gave her hope, but they also made her feel called out and exposed. Could everyone see how desperate she was to be accepted? To be loved?

Mary patted Emma's arm. "But enough about that. Let's get you what you need. I'm thinking purple for you, *ya*? That would be a lovely color for your skin."

An hour passed in a whirlwind of fabric and chatter. Soon they were out the door, arms loaded down with bags of cotton-polyester blends and lightweight flannel. Their next stop was Aunt Fannie's Amish Gift Shop. Emma used to love going there when she was a child. She was glad to see that the building had been renovated since her last visit, when its age had begun to show. The little shop did not have any peeling paint or loose boards anymore. Instead, the tin roof and gingerbread trim reminded her of an adorable pink-and-white Victorian dollhouse. The Millers' big red barn and silver silo stood in the background beside a rambling, white farmhouse. A pond lay in the distance, its surface sparkling in the sun as the blades of a metal windmill slowly turned and creaked in the breeze.

Sadie turned to Emma as they lumbered up the steps of the little porch. "I sell some of my paintings here, and the last time I dropped off my work, Eliza said that they were about to get a shipment of handcrafted baby toys. I couldn't resist asking her to set a few things aside."

"Eliza Zook?" Emma froze. She remembered Eliza—skinny as a rail, with big round glasses, but most importantly, a stickler for the rules. She never broke them. Ever. And she wasn't afraid to tell other people to follow them.

"She's Eliza King, now." Sadie grinned as she pushed open the door and the bell chimed above their heads. "Now that's a *gut* story. It all started with a runaway horse..." Sadie shook her head. "I'll have to tell you all about it later. She married Gabriel King. You remember him?"

"You mean the Gabriel who was so popular?" Sadie must be talking about a different man.

"*Ya. That* Gabriel." Sadie gave her a knowing look. "I know, hard to believe. But they make the perfect couple. They balance each other."

Emma opened her mouth and closed it again. She did not know how to respond to that. Homely, Goody Two-shoes Eliza—the one the other *youngies* made fun of by calling her Eliza the Perfect—had ended up with the boy every girl in the district had dreamed of marrying?

The reality hit hard. Even Eliza Zook had

found love. Everyone Emma knew had found someone. No, not just someone—their *perfect* someone. But the man who Emma had thought was *her* perfect someone had abandoned her.

"We close in seven minutes, at six o'clock sharp," a voice said from behind the rows of handmade Amish gifts. The tone sounded no-nonsense and precise.

"Hi, Eliza, it's Sadie. And I've got Edna with me, along with her niece, Emma."

"*Ach, gut,* there's something I want to say to Emma. I've been waiting for the chance."

Emma stiffened as she heard a chair scrape against the worn wooden floorboards, then footsteps moving from behind an aisle. Eliza appeared from behind a display of faceless Amish dolls. She was as skinny as ever, and still wore her big, round glasses. She pushed them up her narrow nose and stared down at Emma. "I heard you got yourself in the family way during your *Rumspringa* and the *Englischer daed* doesn't want anything to do with you now. We all heard, of course."

Sadie sucked in her breath.

"Eliza, now isn't the time," Edna said quietly.

But Eliza just kept going. "We also heard that you came back to the faith, ain't so?"

Emma swallowed hard and nodded. She

glanced at the door. Could she just run outside and keep running?

"So, that's all wiped clean, but you still need a father for that *boppli*. There's talk that Benjamin is courting you. Is that true?"

"What?" Emma shook her head. *"Nee."*

"Folks said he acted like it at the Hochstetlers' work party. I wasn't there, but you know how word travels."

"I certain sure do," Emma said through gritted teeth.

"There's also talk that you might be trying to take advantage of him. You know, sweet-talk him into marrying you even if it's not a *gut* match."

Emma was stunned. There was so much she wanted to say, but the first words to fly out of her mouth surprised her. "And why wouldn't it be a *gut* match?"

"He might not be ready to be a father. People worry that you might convince him to be one anyway, even if it isn't for the best."

"Is that what you believe?"

"Nee."

"Then why are you telling me this?"

Eliza looked perplexed. "Because I think you ought to know what's being said. It isn't right for people to talk behind your back. But since they are, you have a right to know."

Emma stared at her, unsure how to respond. "Eliza, that's quite enough," Edna said.

Eliza didn't miss a beat. "Now, as for my opinion, I think that you shouldn't listen to what anybody is saying." She leaned forward, cutting the distance between her and Emma. "People talk when they shouldn't. And they act like you did something uniquely terrible. *Vell*, that's a load of nonsense. What you did isn't as bad as what some people—lots of people—do. You just can't hide the evidence. So, it isn't fair and it isn't right for you to get singled out. You know, there's a farmer in the neighboring church district who got caught underpaying and mistreating the men he hired for the harvest. Yet everyone welcomed him back after a short shunning as if it never happened. So why won't they do the same for you?" Eliza moved her hands to her hips. "Don't let them single you out, Emma. Hold your head high."

Emma, Edna, and Sadie all stared at Eliza. The room was so silent that they could hear the creak of the metal windmill outside. Eliza nodded. "*Vell*, that's all I have to say."

"It was a lot," Edna murmured.

"Everyone knows I say what needs to be said," Eliza quipped back.

"You don't mince words, that's for certain sure." Edna rubbed her forehead with her fingertips. "But perhaps you can see that it's better not to bring up things that… Might make the other person uncomfortable."

"Nonsense." Eliza pushed her glasses up her nose. "What's uncomfortable is keeping those things inside. Best said and done. Now, enough of that. Let's get out that box of *boppli* toys I set aside."

When Emma went back to Stoneybrook Farm the next day, Eliza's words were still turning over in her mind. Would Benjamin be embarrassed if he knew that people thought they were courting? Surely, he would be. It was one thing to be her friend, but it was quite another to put himself out there like that. Of course, all that talk was silly anyway. Benjamin could not be interested in her romantically—especially now. He would never want to take on a child that wasn't his. And she would never ask that of him.

Benjamin was waiting in the farmyard when Emma crossed through the gate. He had carried the folding table outside and laid out an assortment of plastic molds, glass vials, milk bottles, measuring cups and spoons, a big mixing bowl, and a cardboard box with the words LYE written on it. He was looking back and forth between the items and a sheet of paper in his hand. His eyes moved to Emma's and he grinned. "I've got everything ready so we can start experimenting."

Something sparked inside Emma's chest. Benjamin had never made her feel that way before. But now, seeing that boyish enthusiasm and genuine smile, something felt right inside. Something happy and bright. Benjamin was so good-natured and fun to be with, so thoughtful and kind. And he always made her laugh. She realized that she was looking forward to spending the afternoon with him.

Emma returned his grin. "*Wunderbar.* Let's get started!"

They spent the next few hours measuring, pouring, and stirring, and experimenting with different essential oil scents. Whenever they had to work with the lye, Benjamin insisted that she stand a few paces away. "I set up outside, instead of in the barn, because the recipes all say that you have to be careful of the fumes. It's best not to be inside an enclosed space." He shifted his weight from one foot to the other. "But, uh, even so, with a, *vell*, you know, women who are… I mean, it's probably best for you not to take any chances."

A few days ago, Emma would have felt called out and shamed. But now, she just felt protected. And, knowing that Benjamin was looking out for her made that warm spark inside her chest flare brighter. "It's *oll recht* to say it out loud." Emma didn't know what compelled her to tell him that. "I'm going to have a *boppli*." Maybe she finally felt safe enough to bring it up. And she didn't want her unborn child to be an elephant in the room that kept her and Benjamin from being real with each other.

Benjamin froze, his hands still on the box of lye. He set down the box slowly and looked up at her with a serious expression. "I've wanted to say something, but I didn't want to make you uncomfortable."

"It's not because you're..." Emma looked down at her hands. She rubbed the bare patch around her finger where Liam should have placed an *Englisch* wedding ring. "Ashamed of me?"

"What?" He stepped back from the table and yanked off his safety glasses. *"Nee."* He shook his head hard as he marched over to her. "Never. I could never—" He stopped short when he reached her, breathing fast. Emma could see the emotion in his eyes. "Please don't think that." His voice was soft but determined. A few beats passed, the only noise the sound of their breathing. Then he cleared his throat. "Sorry, I didn't mean to get so..." He frowned and looked away. *"Vell*, it's important to me, that's all. I want you to know that I don't feel that way. No one should."

"I'm glad you told me."

His eyes jerked back to hers. "You are?"

"Ya."

They stared into one another's eyes for a moment, unsure of what to say.

"Hey, Benji!" A shout came from across the yard. "Can you help me with this?"

They both turned to see Miriam hauling a crate of glass bottles filled with frothy white milk.

Benjamin hesitated.

"It's heavy, Benji. I don't want to drop it."

Benjamin sighed. "I'll be back in a minute," he said before jogging away.

Emma was left standing alone, her heart pounding from the conversation that had been cut short. Why it was pounding, she wasn't quite sure. But Benjamin's intensity had stirred something within her.

He had meant what he said.

Emma glanced over to see Benjamin take the crate from Miriam. Her expression was sharp and guarded. Emma looked away. She didn't want them to think that she was watching them. But, when she heard the low murmur of their voices, she couldn't help but listen. The wind carried Benji's voice, and Emma strained to make out the words. "This isn't heavy at all." Or that's what she thought he said, anyway. It was hard to make out. "You carry stuff a lot heavier than this all the time," he continued.

ach, vell, I'm not as young as I used to be."

"You just turned thirty," Benjamin said.

Miriam grunted.

Emma was glad she couldn't hear the rest of the conversation. It seemed pretty obvious that Miriam had timed her sudden weakness strategically. So she wasn't surprised when Miriam kept appearing throughout the rest of the afternoon, especially when Emma and Benjamin were deep in conversation. At those moments, Miriam suddenly had to take the clothes off the line, or check on the goats, or sweep the steps. By the end of their time together, Benjamin kept glancing over at his sister with an irritated expression. He didn't say anything to Emma, but he didn't have to. Emma knew exactly what was going on. And every time she glanced up to see Miriam's sharp, dark eyes watching them, the shame crept back inside her.

Chapter Eight

~

The next day, Emma strolled through the gate, shut and latched it behind her, and waved at Benjamin. She looked radiant as the afternoon sun highlighted her honey-blond hair and surrounded her in a warm glow. He wanted to race to her and tell her how beautiful she was, but that would be unfair. He was her friend and that was what she needed right now—a friend. He wouldn't risk that friendship by letting her know how deep his feelings really went. She meant too much to him for that.

Ollie trotted past Benjamin, loped over to Emma, and sniffed her hand. "Hey, Ollie," she murmured and patted him on the head. He watched her through cautious eyes, circled her once, then wandered away, nose to the ground, ears alert.

Benjamin knew he needed to tell her right away. He took a deep breath. "I, uh, made a mistake."

"Oh. What happened?" Emma lifted the blade

of her hand to her forehead and squinted into the sun to study his expression. "Are you *oll recht*?"

"*Ya, ya.* I'm fine. It's just that I got mixed up and didn't realize how long the soap will take to cure. We won't be able to sell it for three weeks."

Emma shrugged. "That's not a big deal."

Benjamin felt the tension leave his neck and shoulders. He had not realized how tight they had been. He just wanted Emma to see that he was competent. It seemed like she was the only person who ever had. But they weren't children anymore, and he didn't expect her to have the same patience with him that she once had. She would expect him to do better now that he was a man. "You don't think so?"

"*Nee.*"

"What about, uh…" He fiddled with one of his black suspenders. "Your due date? You should probably start resting up pretty soon? Stay off your feet, *ya*?"

"I'd rather stay busy."

"Me too," Benjamin said. "When I don't have enough to do, I get to thinking, and then, *vell*…" He shook his head. It was better not to say any more. "Sometimes it's best not to think too much."

"That's exactly how I feel too."

Benjamin wanted to tell her that thoughts of *her* were what troubled him. He worried about her and her baby. Now that she was expecting, the feelings he had always had for her were only growing stronger. He wanted to take care of her. He wanted to offer to be a father to her child— to stand with them, love and support them. But that wasn't his place. She might still be in love with the biological father, for all Benjamin knew. "*Vell*, let's keep you busy, then. I've found a way to make soap that doesn't take long to cure."

"You've been doing a lot of research."

Benjamin shrugged off the compliment, but couldn't hide his smile. "I've spent some time reading."

"A lot of time, certain sure."

"*Oll recht.* A lot of time. I've checked out three more books from the library. And I bought another one at the bookstore downtown. I think we have all the information we need now."

"And if we don't, that's okay. We'll just try again."

Benjamin jerked his head around to look at her. "You mean that?"

"Of course." Emma grinned. "So how do we get started?"

Benjamin had bought a slow cooker from the general store in downtown Blueberry Hills and set it up in the production building, where a generator provided power. He wished they could work in the barn, away from his sisters, but there was no power source there. So he led Emma across the yard, behind the farmhouse, and across a damp patch of bare earth the goats had picked clean, to a building with corrugated sheet metal walls and a concrete foundation. "Right in here," he said as he held the big double doors open for her.

The familiar rush of cool air and whir of machinery met them as they entered the building. Emma glanced around. "This is a nice setup. You've updated since the last time I was in here."

"I'm glad you like it. Some church districts might say it's too fancy, but Bishop Amos and the elders agree that its *oll recht* to use the generator and the equipment because it's for business only. Silas and Mary Hochstetler power the sewing machines for their harness business the same way."

Emma nodded. Benjamin watched as she studied the shiny metal vats and coils. He wondered what it would be like to see her in here, every day, working side by side with him—

No. He could not let himself dream those dreams. Emma was not interested in him. How could she be? Some folks might whisper that she was unmarriageable now, but he knew that was ridiculous. There would be men lining up to propose—men with a lot more to offer than he ever could. She was like a dancing ray of light, impossible to contain. Her circumstances had dulled her sparkle, but it would come back and when it did, so would the suitors. All she had to do was put herself out there, and that would be that. In the meantime, he would just have to appreciate what little time he had left with her. The memory of these happy afternoons together would have to be enough.

"You've already got it all set up." Emma saw the slow cooker on a long, gray counter and made a beeline for it. Benjamin pulled milk bottles from the freezer. The glass door thumped shut behind him as he padded across the concrete floor to the counter. "I put these in earlier today. The milk is supposed to be slushy." He held up a bottle and studied the contents. "Looks about right, *ya*?"

"*Ya.*"

"We should have everything we need here." Benjamin scanned the supplies, then nodded. He hoped he had not forgotten anything. That would just prove to Emma that he couldn't manage on his own. It was bad enough that he needed help with the sums. "I brought the accounting book in here too so we can figure the cost of the slow cooker and the recipe book into the budget." By *we* he meant *you*, but *we* sounded a lot better. Benjamin waited for that pitying glance that his older sisters would have given him, but Emma just gave a quick, decisive nod. "Got it."

They measured out the coconut oil, olive oil, and castor oil and poured it all into the slow cooker to melt. After they measured the milk into a bowl, Benjamin stepped back from the counter. "I'm going to take it outside to add the lye. We're not taking any risks with that *boppli*."

He hoped that he hadn't said too much, but after yesterday's conversation he was pretty confident that she wouldn't be offended if he pointed out the facts. The way her face lit up confirmed it. "*Danki*, Benji." Emma looked down, but the smile lingered on her face. "I really appreciate the way you look out for me—for us."

Benjamin's heart took off in a little dance. She appreciated him. The idea filled him with an easy warmth and put an extra spring in his step as he walked away.

"I'll catch up on the arithmetic while you're gone," Emma said while he was still within earshot. He glanced back to smile, forgot to watch where he was going, bumped into a rolling cart filled with glass bottles, and nearly dropped the bowl of milk in his hands. He caught his balance and righted himself just in time, while somehow managing to keep the milk from sloshing over the side of the bowl. But the cart rolled across the floor from the impact and bumped into a metal vat. The glass bottles rattled against one another when the cart hit, sending a clatter echoing through the room. He flinched and snuck another glance at Emma.

She shot him a good-natured grin. He sensed that she was laughing with him, not at him, and he slowly relaxed. "I keep bumping into everything too," she said. "I nearly shut the door on my belly the other day. Can't seem to remember how much more of me there is now."

Benjamin laughed. "I've always bumped into things. Guess we're finally alike that way." Was it okay that he said that? He hoped she understood what he meant.

"*Ya.* And I'm always dropping things now—and forgetting things too. I didn't know having a *boppli* would do that to me." Emma frowned. "Sorry, it's not like what you've always had to deal with. I just want you to know that it's easier to understand now. I guess I always took things for granted before, back when everything worked the way I wanted it to. Now, I couldn't imagine doing things that used to be easy, like playing volleyball."

"*Vell*, then we can sit out together, ain't so?" Benjamin had spent his time in youth group making up excuses to get out of playing. He couldn't admit to the other *youngies* that he didn't have the coordination to keep up with them. How could they understand when he looked like there was nothing wrong?

Emma smiled, but there was a wistful sadness behind her eyes. Benjamin realized he had said the wrong thing. Emma could never go to another youth group meeting. She was no longer one of them. But she wasn't one of the married folks, either. She was in a category all her own, with no one to stand with her. The realization made Benjamin ache inside. He stared at her and swallowed. How could he put his feelings into words?

He couldn't. So he nodded, then turned away to head outside.

As soon as Benjamin disappeared around the other side of the big metal vats, Emma picked up the pencil on the counter and began to flip through the accounting book. She scanned the neat row of numbers that she had written earlier, tapped the page with the end of the pencil, and began to subtract in her head. There was a whoosh as the doors opened. Emma couldn't see who was there, on the other side of the equipment, but she could hear the voices. Miriam and Naomi. "*Ya*, I was worried too," Naomi said. There was the sound of the door thudding shut, followed by footsteps. Emma wondered if she should say something so they knew she was there, but that felt unnecessary. They would see her as soon as they came around the equipment.

"You're not worried anymore?" Miriam asked.

"*Nee.* Benji's got a *gut* head on his shoulders, in spite of everything. He just doesn't know how to explain himself."

"True. He can't put his thoughts into words."

"But I'm certain sure he knows that Emma is all wrong for him," Naomi said.

"I hope you're right. Can you imagine what a marriage like that would be like for him? A *boppli* and a scandal? How would he handle it?"

Emma flinched. She should have said something earlier. Now it was too late. She sat very still and hoped that they couldn't hear her breathing.

"Emma's a sweet girl," Naomi said.

Emma was surprised to hear that, though it did little to take away the sting.

"I'm not saying she isn't," Miriam said.

"She just can't seem to stay out of trouble."

"Never could."

"I just didn't think she'd get into *this* kind of trouble," Naomi said.

"*Ya.* It's one thing to be a careless *kinner*, going a little too far with pranks and fun, but this is something else entirely. I know Leah thinks I'm being too hard on Emma, but I just don't want to see her drag Benji down with her. What if she ends up jumping the fence again?"

"I've thought about that," Naomi said. There was a metallic clang followed by the click of a dial turning. "But I don't think it will happen. She wouldn't have come back to the faith in the first place, if she were going to do that."

"I hope you're right," Miriam said.

"She'll make a *gut fraa* for someone one day," Naomi said.

"Just not for our Benji. He's too trusting. And what really happened with the father? We don't know. What if he tries to *kumme* back in the picture? *Nee*, it's just too much for Benji to take on." There was a heavy sigh. "I know he thinks I'm being callous. I care about Emma, I really do. It's just that our brother has to be my priority. It's up to me to make sure he has a *gut* future."

"That's not all on you. You know that."

Miriam grunted. "*Oll recht*. It's up to *Gott*. You're right. But I still have to do everything I can."

"While you trust *Gott*."

"*Ya.*"

"Don't forget that part, Miriam."

There was a long pause. "I won't. But it isn't always easy. Once I know that Benji is *oll recht*, I'll finally be able to relax for the first time in twelve years."

"Remember what I said. Benji isn't interested in marrying into a ready-made family. He's too carefree for that. He's not ready to settle down with a baby. He won't be persuaded by Emma. I really don't think you need to worry."

"I'm sure you're right. But you know it isn't easy to stop worrying."

Footsteps echoed against the high ceiling, but the sound was moving away from Emma.

"Grab the milk we came for," Miriam said. "We need to get going. They'll be back in here soon." There was a thud and a thump, the clatter of glass against glass, then more footsteps, followed by the soft whoosh of the door opening. After that, the room was silent again, except for the quiet hum of machinery.

Emma let out her breath. She had not realized that she had been holding it. She sat on the stool, stunned, unable to move for a moment. Her first instinct was to run outside, shake her fist, and defend herself.

But the truth was, she believed that they were right.

She *had* always gotten in trouble. But it had always been little things before. *Englischers,* who weren't as strict about these things, would have probably just called her mischievous or free-spirited. But this was different. She had crossed an

uncrossable line. This was something that could
never be undone.

How could she even consider that Benjamin might be interested in a future with her? It
wasn't just unlikely, it was selfish. He deserved
his own life, his own dreams. She shouldn't drag
him into her problems.

And yet, the warm, happy feeling she felt inside when she thought about him wouldn't go
away. She had not considered that it could be
love—or anything close to love. Surely it wasn't.
But it was something more than friendship. He
had an honesty and a depth to him that no one
else had. He was selfless and kind like no other
man she knew.

Which was exactly why she shouldn't let herself run away with foolish thoughts about his
being a good father. That kind of dream was
for women like Sadie, Eliza, and Mary. Women
who followed the rules, did everything right, and
were rewarded.

That was not the woman she was. And no one
would ever let her forget it.

Perhaps they never should.

Emma jumped when she heard the door open
and Benjamin's footsteps bounded across the
concrete floor. He was moving fast and she
could sense his happiness. She owed it to him
not to spoil it.

He rounded the big metal vat, held up the bowl, and grinned. "*Oll recht*, next step."

Emma forced a smile. She would enjoy their friendship for as long as she could. He would need to get a *fraa* someday. A *gut* match who would not drag him down. She was surprised that he wasn't already courting someone. It was true that he had never been popular, but he would be a very good catch.

Emma frowned. Benjamin, a good catch? That was a thought that would have never crossed her mind before now. But he was. And anyone who couldn't see it was simply blind to reality.

"Emma?" Benji stood in front of her. "What's the matter?"

"*Ach*, I'm fine." Her hand instinctively went to her belly for comfort. Hearing what Miriam and Naomi had said about her, then thinking of Benjamin with a wife, it was all too much.

Benjamin's gaze shot to her belly and his eyes widened. "You're having contractions. I'll get help."

"*Nee*." Emma shook her head. She couldn't stop from smiling when she saw how concerned he looked. It made her feel loved. She shoved the thought away. Naomi had confirmed what Emma had already known—that Benjamin could never be interested in her that way. "I'm not having contractions."

"Oh." Benjamin stood still for a moment. "Then what's the matter?"

"Nothing, really. I'm *oll recht*."

"I know you better than that. It's okay to tell me." He cleared his throat and focused on the bowl in his hands. "I mean, only if you want to. You don't have to say anything." He set the bowl down on the counter. "It's not something I did, is it?" He did not look at her.

"*Nee*. It's nothing like that. I just have a lot to think about."

He let out a breath of air. "*Gut*. I mean, it's not *gut* that you have a lot to think about, just that—"

"I know what you mean."

Benjamin flashed a smile. "You've always gotten me when other people didn't, you know."

Emma felt a twisting inside her chest that was as real as physical pain. "And you've always gotten me." For the first time, Emma wondered what could have happened between them, if things had been different. Why had she never seen Benjamin for who he really was before? He had always been this kind, this insightful, this gentle. She looked at his face and realized that he had always been this handsome too. The high, defined cheekbones, the straight nose and full lips. The dark features. Tall, dark and handsome, she'd heard the *Englischers* say. Benjamin? Her

Benjamin? Tall, dark and handsome, like a character from a romance novel?

Yes. He was. She just had not seen it before, because he had always been there, as solid and reliable as the land their families farmed. She had overlooked him.

And now that she finally saw him, it was too late.

Chapter Nine

That Saturday, Emma could almost forget the despair she had felt the last time she and Benjamin were together. They were headed to the farmers market and Benjamin's grin lit the way. The look on his face pulled Emma out of her pain and reminded her that life could be light-hearted and fun again.

"Walk on," he said and slapped the reins. "Clyde's a *gut* old horse, but he's slow as molasses. It's fine for a visiting Sunday when you just want to relax, but I can't wait to get to the market today."

Emma returned his grin. "I can't wait, either." That was one of the things that was so refreshing about Benjamin. He never tried to hide his enthusiasm. He wasn't like the boys she used to hang out with who hid their excitement to prove how cool and tough they were. Benjamin didn't seem to care if anyone knew that he was happy or excited. And that meant that his joy spread to everyone around him.

Liam had been the opposite of that. He rarely smiled. She remembered his serious expression as he tapped his finger on the steering wheel of his car in time with the bass that blasted from the stereo system. And he certainly wasn't smiling on that terrible day when Emma had to tell him that he was going to be a father.

"No, I'm not," he had said. And that was it. Three simple words and everything shattered. Emma thought she would never smile again, either.

And then she reconnected with Benjamin.

He hummed a tune from the *Ausbund* as the buggy wheels clattered over the pavement and Clyde's hooves thudded in a slow rhythm. "Not too much longer, now," he said and flashed her another smile. "How much do you think we'll sell?"

"All of it."

His smile widened to his signature grin. "You really think so?"

"I really do. You had *wunderbar* ideas. I think I like the lavender birchwood-scented soap best. But your rosemary lemon smells really *gut* too. And the mint."

"It was your idea to add in the sprigs of real lavender, rosemary, and mint."

Emma winked. "I'm smart like that, ain't so?"

"For certain sure."

Emma gave him a playful punch on the arm. "I was joking. I'm not that prideful."

Benjamin shrugged. He was still smiling. "I know. But it just happens to be true."

There was an awkward silence. Something crackled in the air between them. But Emma remembered she shouldn't let herself feel that bright, happy spark. She had to extinguish it, or she would end up humiliating herself, or even worse, stealing Benjamin's future from him. "Hey look." She pointed down the highway. "We're here."

A long wooden building stood alongside the road. The walls were painted red and the tin roof had a cupola on top with a rooster weathervane, giving a vague impression of a barn. A big sign across the front read "Blueberry Hills Farmers Market." The parking lot was already a quarter full with cars, pickup trucks, and buggies. Trunks, truck beds, and buggy doors hung open as vendors pulled out their wares. Two teenaged girls stood in the bed of a blue pickup truck, passing rocking chairs down to their father. An Amish woman pulled a little red wagon filled with homemade pies as she called for her children to follow. Some vendors were setting up beneath wooden shelters on the front lawn, while others carried crates inside the building.

"I reserved us a booth beneath that shelter."

Emma nodded toward one of the wooden structures.

Benjamin tugged the reins and the buggy veered off the highway and into the parking lot. Gravel crunched beneath the wheels. "*Danki* for taking care of that."

"That's what I'm here for."

"*Ya.*"

But Emma knew that, in her heart, she was here for more than that. She was here as Benjamin's friend. Or maybe something more that she could not allow herself to feel, even though it pulsed inside her chest, asking to be heard.

She glanced over and saw that Benjamin was frowning. She wondered why. It couldn't be that he was thinking the same thing, could it? Maybe he wanted their time together to be more than just a business arrangement too.

Or maybe he was just concentrating on navigating the crowd as he drove the buggy. She shouldn't jump to silly conclusions or make up connections that weren't there.

"Whoa," Benjamin said. The buggy slowed to a stop in the overflow field just beyond the gravel lot. Clyde swished his tail and lowered his head to sample the grass. Benjamin pulled the handbrake. "I'll get everything unloaded." But instead of heading directly to the back of the buggy, he jogged around to Emma's side and helped her down. He looked bashful when he offered his hand. "Hope you don't mind," he murmured. "I just don't want you to stumble."

Emma beamed. "Of course I don't mind. *Danki.*" Liam had never opened doors for her or helped her out of the car. She had forgotten what it was like to feel special. As Benjamin's big, calloused hand touched hers, a sensation like electricity pulsed up her arm and hit her heart. She wanted his hand to stay on hers, strong and comforting. But as soon as her feet touched the ground, he released her hand so quickly that it felt like she had imagined it all. He avoided making eye contact with her and she wondered if he wished that he hadn't touched her. Or maybe he felt as shaken by the encounter as she did?

Emma tried to push down her feelings as she followed him to the back of the buggy. "I can grab the cardboard box. It's light enough."

"Absolutely not. I'll carry everything. It will only take me one or two trips. I'll meet you over at the shelter."

"*Vell,* in that case, how about I grab us some pumpkin spice lattes? I bet they've got them for sale inside."

Benjamin grinned. "It's that time of year again. That's one thing the *Englischers* do right, ain't so?" He winked at her and added, "But don't tell my sisters I said that."

Emma laughed. "I won't. But you're right."

"Here." He pulled out a few bills and handed them to her. "My treat."

Emma hesitated. It almost felt like a date.

Benjamin raised his eyebrows. "Go on and take it. You're not paying. That would be *lecherich*."

Emma wanted to respond that it was ridiculous for her to take money from him when she was supposed to be working for him. This was all business. Until suddenly, it wasn't. She could feel it. And she knew he could too. He shifted his weight from one foot to the other and waited.

"Danki," she said as she took the money. "I'll get you a large."

"You'd better. Because you'll just have to get a second one for me later, if you get a small. And maybe grab us each a pumpkin whoopie pie, if they've got any."

Liam would never have admitted that he liked pumpkin spice anything. Too girlie, he would have said. But Benjamin wasn't insecure like that. He didn't have to make a big show of being a man. He could just be himself, without hiding who he was. Because he *was* a real man. Suddenly, Emma realized that she was impressed by Benjamin. He was purely, unapologetically himself. Sure, he seemed insecure about his disabilities, but he never overcompensated by trying to prove how tough and strong he could be. And *that* was true strength.

Emma found herself smiling as she walked inside the big building and headed to the bakery counter near the entrance. The scent of cinnamon rolls and fresh-brewed coffee hung in the air, mingling with the hum of conversation from the crowd.

When she walked back outside with two pumpkin spice lattes and two whoopie pies, the bright blue autumn sky welcomed her. Everything felt crisp and clear, with a hint of cool air that made her glad that she had worn a black sweater over her emerald green cape dress. She saw Benjamin carrying a crate toward the shelter. He noticed her, turned his attention her way, and nodded. As soon as his eyes moved away from the ground, his feet slipped over a patch of loose gravel. In an instant, his expression changed to surprise as he rocketed forward, stumbled to regain his balance, and lost his grip on the crate. It crashed to the ground in a loud thwack that made Emma cringe. The bars of soap bounced out of the crate and crashed against a concrete bumper at the edge of the parking lot.

Benjamin managed to stay upright, but the look on his face showed that he would have rather sacrificed himself than the soap. He crouched down and examined the bars scattered across the ground. They had wrapped each one in tissue paper, tied a piece of twine around it, and attached a brown paper label with the ingredients written on it in Emma's neat cursive. Benjamin sucked in his breath through his teeth. "I broke them."

Emma rushed forward. "I'm sure it's fine."

Benjamin looked up at her and shook his head. "*Nee.* They're ruined." The look on his face broke Emma's heart. She could see the embarrassment and shame in his eyes. She wanted to take him in her arms and tell him that it was okay, that she didn't think any less of him. That she only saw how hard he worked, how much effort he made. His refusal to quit was what impressed her, not the mistakes he made along the way. How many men had she known who puffed out their chests and made a big show of being strong and athletic, but never made any effort beyond that? They didn't try because they didn't have to. But Benjamin had not had anything handed to him, so he took nothing for granted. He never showed off. He was humble—truly humble in the way an Amish man should be. Few men actually lived up to that standard, even though they loved to talk about it as though they did.

Benjamin picked up the bars from the ground and set them back in the crate, one by one. He handled them gently, even though they were already broken and it was too late. "Do you want to leave?" he asked without looking up at her.

"Leave? Absolutely not. I want to enjoy this pumpkin spice latte with you and sell whatever we can."

Benjamin sighed and stood up. "I don't think we can sell much of this anymore. I should have made the bars thicker. And I might have gotten the recipe wrong. They're too brittle. They all cracked when they hit the concrete."

"It's *oll recht*. We'll just have to be creative. Let's sell the broken bars on discount. We won't make a profit, but maybe we can break even." She flashed him an encouraging smile. "It'll be *gut* advertising. Customers will come back for more and next time they'll pay full price." Emma walked alongside Benjamin as he carried the crate to the shelter and set it down on the folding table that he had set up while she was buying coffee. "Whatever is too broken to sell on discount, we'll give away as free samples. More *gut* advertising."

Benjamin stared at the crate and nodded. "You're smart, Emma. That's not a bad idea."

"Are you kidding? It's a brilliant idea."

Benjamin laughed and Emma felt good that she had cheered him up.

"Can you make a sign that says free samples?

You know how bad my handwriting is." He glanced around and frowned. "Wait. We didn't bring anything to use for a sign."

"Not a problem. I'll tear the flap off the cardboard box and use it. It's just the right size. And I threw some permanent markers in the box with the accounting book. We've got this."

Benjamin nodded. His brow still had that crinkle of concern and he was having trouble meeting her eyes, but he didn't hide that shame behind anger, like a weaker man would have done. Instead, he just started unpacking the crate, carefully arranging each bar into neat rows. He never shifted the blame onto her. He didn't try to shut down his emotions. He just shrugged and smiled and got on with it.

She had never admired anyone more.

Benjamin wanted the earth to swallow him up whole. He could not believe that he had ruined their chance to make a profit today. Worse, Emma had watched the entire humiliating episode. He had wanted so badly to impress her.

Thankfully, she was too gracious to say anything bad about the situation. Instead, she made everything better with that upbeat, indomitable spirit of hers. That was the Emma he had always known. The Emma that couldn't be stopped, that didn't see obstacles, only challenges to be overcome. He smiled to himself. Maybe it wasn't so bad that he had fallen down and ruined everything. If it helped Emma find herself again, then it was worth it.

"What are you thinking about?" Emma asked. "You're smiling."

"Oh." He cleared his throat and took a sip of his pumpkin spice latte. It was too hot and he burned his tongue. He grimaced and put down the paper cup. "I was just feeling *gut* about things, I guess."

Emma looked surprised, but pleased. Benjamin wondered how she really felt about being here with him. They had settled back into their old, familiar camaraderie. But, if he didn't know any better, he could almost believe that there was something more forming between them. When she looked at him, he saw that flicker behind her eyes—as if she sensed a connection—and liked it.

He slipped the lid off his cup and blew across the top of the coffee to cool it. "Guess there's nothing to do but wait, now."

Emma peeled the plastic wrap off her whoopie pie. "And eat. This will not be my only dessert of the day. I can promise you that."

Benjamin chuckled. "Sounds *gut* to me."

Car doors slammed in the distance. "The market's open," Emma said. She sat up straighter and studied the crowds forming in the parking lot. She suddenly looked nervous and vulnerable. Benjamin wondered if she was worried about running into people from the church district. He wished he could throw his arm around her, pull her toward him, and tell her that it would be okay and that he would stand up for her, no matter what.

He was still trying to figure out what to say and how to say it when a customer wandered up to their booth. She wore a red dress and brown leather boots that matched her handbag. Her blond hair was swept into a messy ponytail. She looked middle aged, early fifties, probably. "Goat milk soap?" she asked.

"Ya," Benjamin said. "We make it by hand on my goat farm."

"How quaint." The woman picked up a bar and held it to her nose. "Mmm. Lavender." She went down the row, examining the different bars. "Is this all you have?"

Benjamin shifted in his folding chair. *"Vell,* we have some damaged bars on discount. And the free samples." He pointed to a small stack of soap. "That's all we have right now at full price."

"Oh. Okay." She picked up a bar of rosemary lemon and read the label. "I hear goat milk is good for eczema. Is that true? Most soap that I try only makes it worse."

"*Ya.* It's true for certain sure. Try a free sample and see if it works for you. If it does you can *kumme* back for more."

"Thanks. That's a good idea." She sifted through the basket of broken bits of soap, plucked out a few large pieces, and walked away.

"You're a *gut* man, Benjamin."

"What?"

"You could have made a sale, if you had pushed for it. But instead, you encouraged her to try it for free first."

"*Vell,* it wouldn't be right to sell her soap that hurts her skin. She ought to try it out first."

"That's true. But not everyone would think that way. They would care more about making a sale."

Benjamin shrugged. "Guess I'm not much of a salesman."

Emma smiled and there was something wistful behind her eyes. "*Nee.* You're something better."

Benjamin wanted to ask her what she meant by that. But another woman stopped by the booth before he could say anything. She looked to be in her sixties, or seventies maybe, and wore a sensible pair of cotton pants with a matching cardigan. She pushed her sunglasses onto the top of her head and smiled at Emma. "When is the baby due?"

Emma's posture deflated and her hand went to her belly. "Um, not much longer now."

"No, I bet not. You look ready to burst. I carried like that too. As if I swallowed a watermelon. I bet people tell you that all the time."

Emma managed a strained smile. *"Ya."*

"You look like such a nice couple. I'll take four, no five bars of soap. I'd much rather give you my business than the big-box store down the street." She pulled a leather wallet out of her bag, riffled through it, and handed a stack of bills to Benjamin. Then she unsnapped a coin purse, picked out an assortment of nickels, dimes, and pennies, and dropped them into his palm. "Is that enough?"

"Uh, let me see…"

"Here, I'll take care of that while you bag the soap." Emma swept the money out of Benjamin's hand before he could say anything. She had rescued him from another moment of embarrassment. He snuck her a quick smile, which she returned, before she began counting the money. It flew through her fingers quickly and, just like that, she was finished. "Here." She handed a nickel back to the woman. "You overpaid."

The woman dropped the nickel into her coin purse and snapped it shut, then said to Benjamin, "I'll take an assortment."

"Sounds *gut*."

"You two look so young," the woman said as Benjamin placed the bars of tissue-wrapped soap into a white paper bag. "You must be new-lyweds."

Emma looked like she wanted to disappear under the table.

"You're right, we are pretty young." Benjamin thought that was a good save. He would not humiliate Emma by pointing out that they weren't married—that she wasn't married to anyone. But, of course, he wouldn't outright lie, either.

"Never too young to be in love."

Benjamin cleared his throat. This was getting sticky. He was afraid his true feelings for Emma would show on his face. It was as if the woman had seen right through him to how he really felt.

Emma straightened a bar of soap on the table and refused to look at either of them.

Benjamin folded the bag shut and handed it to the woman. He would have to move her along before this became too embarrassing for Emma. "All the ingredients are listed on the label," he said quickly. "*Danki* for buying so many bars. We hope you enjoy your purchase. Take care."

"And you take good care of that sweet wife of yours."

"I will." That was not a lie. Emma wasn't his wife, but he *would* take care of her. He wanted nothing more in the world.

Chapter Ten

Emma wanted to sink into the trampled grass beneath the folding table and disappear beneath the earth. What must Benjamin be thinking right now? It had to offend an upright Amish man like him to be mistaken for her husband. The more the *Englischer* woman had talked, the more Emma had felt the shame imprinted on her cheeks. Surely everyone could see it. Her skin must still be as red as a beet.

And through it all, Benjamin had just smiled politely at the woman and said exactly the right thing. He had rescued her. Again. It was becoming a habit of his, one that made Emma feel lightheaded and breathless.

Maybe that swoony excitement was just anxiety and pregnancy. That made more sense. Otherwise, how could she explain the exhilaration she felt at the thought of being Benjamin's newlywed wife? That joy collided with the shame she felt, making it hard to grasp what was happening.

They did not acknowledge the awkward conversation, of course. Benjamin avoided her eyes for a long time, and when they finally fell back into their usual easy, lighthearted conversation, they both pretended that the entire incident had never happened. It was easier that way. If Emma said anything—if she thanked Benjamin for letting the woman assume they were married—that would just highlight the fact that she had no father for this baby. And her due date was approaching fast. The fact that more strangers made comments about her belly throughout the day kept reminding her that the clock was ticking. By the time afternoon rolled around, she had heard more than enough.

Emma's hand moved down to her belly and she felt the baby shift toward her palm. Her baby. Nothing could be so sweet and precious. The yearning and love formed an ache in her chest. *You deserve a* daed. *A* gut *Amish* daed *like Benjamin.* She didn't try to push away the thought this time. It didn't even feel ridiculous anymore.

It was starting to feel just right.

"*Vell*, I guess it's time to pack up," Benjamin said.

Emma startled and sat up straight. "Right." She caught a hint of concern in his expression as she tossed the accounting book into a box. "Is everything *oll recht*?"

Benjamin picked up a bar of discounted soap and set it inside the crate. "*Ya*. Everything's *gut*."

Emma raised her eyebrows and gave him a no-nonsense look. "I know when something's eating at you. What is it?"

"*Ach, vell*, we didn't earn as much as we should have. You had a *gut* idea to sell these bars on discount and we sold a lot of them. But we barely broke even." He shook his head. "I cost us our profit."

Emma stood up and collected the cardboard sign that read "Free Samples" and the empty basket. "Today was all about marketing. We got the word out. People will come back next time, and when they do, they'll pay full price." She nudged him with her shoulder. "It's going to work out, I promise."

Benjamin nodded, but he didn't look convinced. He looked like he was about to say something, but instead he finished stacking the bars of soap inside the crate, picked it up, and started for the buggy. He paused and turned back around. "How do you know that?"

Emma wondered if she could tell him the truth. Would he think that she was too forward? Would he think that she was trying to sweet-talk him into marrying her? Wasn't that what everyone else thought? She swallowed hard and decided to be brave, because he deserved to hear the truth. "Because I believe in you."

Benjamin stared at her. Emma could see the tick of his pulse in his throat, hear the quick rasp of his breath. The parking lot felt very far away, as if it were only them, alone in the field. "You do?" he asked finally.

"Ya," she said. Her voice was quiet, almost a whisper. "I always have." Their eyes stayed locked on one another. "Even when we stopped hanging out, I still believed in you. You've always been a *gut* man, Benjamin Stoltzfus."

"You...think that about me?"

"How could I think anything else?"

Benjamin kept staring at her. Energy zipped between them. Emma felt weak and strong at the same time, like she might faint or jump right into his arms. Something was happening between them.

It was Benjamin who finally broke eye contact. He looked down and rubbed the back of his neck. "You've always been my friend. My best friend." His eyes moved back up to hers, just for a moment, then away again. Silence. Emma waited for him to say more. But instead, he adjusted his grip on the crate and headed toward the buggy. "Better get everything loaded," he called out as he walked away.

Emma sank back against the metal folding

chair. Had she just imagined the entire inter-action? She shifted uneasily on the cushion—the cushion that Benjamin had brought to make her more comfortable. Another one of his small, thoughtful gestures. After so many thoughtful gestures, she had begun to allow a small, unspo-ken hope. And hadn't they just shared a connec-tion that validated that hope?

No, she had gotten it wrong. He had made sure to tell her that he saw her as a friend. *Only* as a friend. Sweet, thoughtful Benjamin. He would be careful. He would tiptoe around the truth to save her from the humiliation. He didn't want to hurt her feelings. But she got the message. She got it loud and clear.

What she didn't understand was why it hurt so badly. Wasn't this how things were supposed to be? She and Benjamin, good, old, reliable friends. Nothing more.

Somehow, without her realizing it, her feel-ings had shifted into a love that could no longer be stuffed down and ignored.

Love?

Was it possible?

No, it couldn't be. Emma squinted into the dis-tance and watched Benjamin patting Clyde on the shoulder before he doubled back to her. His walk was so familiar, his quick smile so com-forting as he cut through the field.

Whatever this feeling was, she could not allow it. He had made that clear. She would shut it down, for his sake. And somehow, she would manage to stay his friend, even as she longed for something more. His friendship was too precious to lose.

Benjamin could not stop humming when he got home. Emma believed in him. She had said it out loud, clear as day. And he had risked everything to tell her how he felt in return. *You've always been my friend. My best friend.* He had been so afraid to say it out loud that he had barely been able to make eye contact with her. But he had said it. He had all but declared his love for her.

Okay, he hadn't told her that he loved her, not exactly. He couldn't put her on the spot like that. But he had let her know how much she meant to him—how much she had always meant to him. And that was important. Maybe she was thinking of him right now, feeling secure in their relationship, in how much he cared about her. She wouldn't feel alone anymore. That had been worth the risk to say the words out loud.

"Hey, Benji, watch out."

"Huh?" His attention jerked toward Leah's voice.

"I just mopped the floor."

"Oh. Right."

"Don't worry about it. It'll be dirty again in five

minutes anyway. This floor is a magnet for mud. We may as well just let the goats come right in."

"Miriam might have something to say about that."

Leah giggled and shook her head.

He kicked off his boots and left them in the hallway, just outside the kitchen door, then padded across the linoleum and pulled a glass bottle of fresh goat milk from the propane-powered refrigerator.

"I'd say everything went well by the look on your face," Leah said.

Benjamin grinned, then chugged the milk down in big gulps. After the bottle was half-empty, he pulled it from his lips and wiped his mouth. "You could say that."

Leah raised her eyebrows. "Benji, you've got a twinkle in your eye." She set down the mop, leaned back against the counter, and crossed her arms. "Start talking."

Benjamin shrugged. But he knew it wouldn't do any good to pretend. Hiding his feelings had never been his talent. "It's *gut* to have a friend like Emma, that's all."

Leah glanced toward the hallway and lowered her voice. "Just a friend?" Her expression looked hopeful.

Benjamin smiled and looked down. But he couldn't stop the smile from spreading across his face. "*Ya*. Probably. Maybe... I mean... Let's just say it went well today."

Leah's eyes widened and she scooted closer to him. "Did she say anything? I mean, did she let you know how she feels?"

Benjamin just kept smiling.

"You look like the cat that ate the canary."

"Okay, I don't know what that means. And I don't think I want to."

Leah laughed.

"What I do know is that Emma said she believes in me."

"She—" Leah's attention flicked to the doorway.

Benjamin cleared his throat and straightened up as Miriam and Amanda bustled into the kitchen. "You look happy, Benji," Miriam said.

Benjamin opened the refrigerator and placed the glass bottle back on the shelf.

"*Vell*, don't stop talking just because we came in," Amanda said.

"So, everything went well with the sales today?" Leah asked.

Benji winked at her in a silent thank-you for steering the subject away from Emma. Then he turned back around to face his other sisters. "We sold almost everything."

"*Wunderbar!*" Amanda clapped her hands together. "I'm sorry I doubted you, Benji. We should have known you'd pull through with this. You've always been a hard worker."

Benjamin frowned. "You doubted me?"

Amanda flinched. *"Ach, vell..."* She glanced at Miriam.

Miriam looked annoyed. *"Ya.* A little bit. New business ventures are always risky, even if they're small. You didn't put a lot of capital into it, but the cost of supplies still added up. We weren't sure it would be worth it. Every penny counts around here." Miriam strode over to the counter and pulled out the old, faded recipe book from its place beneath the cabinets. "But we were proud of you for trying. Even if it didn't work out, we would still be proud of you." She opened the book and began to flip through the pages.

Benjamin sighed. He knew Miriam was being supportive, but it felt condescending. It was something a mother could get away with saying, but Miriam wasn't his mother.

"Anyway, I'm glad you made the money back that we put into it. That's a *gut* start."

"I didn't say we made the money back."

Miriam marked her place with her index finger and looked up from the recipe book. "You said it went well."

Benjamin shrugged. "Those can be two different things."

"*Oll recht*, but you understand that you have to make a profit for this to make sense, right?"

"Miriam, of course I understand. I'm a grown man. I know how the world works."

Miriam slammed the book shut, set it down on the counter, and closed her eyes.

The only sound was Amanda putting on a clean work apron. The starched fabric whispered in the tense silence.

Miriam opened her eyes and looked at Benji. "I'm sorry. Of course you know how the world works. I didn't mean it to sound that way."

"You never do," Benjamin mumbled. He had wanted to show Miriam how capable he was. If he had sold everything at the original prices that Emma had set, then he could have proved that. But, of course, he wasn't capable. He had messed up, as usual, and ruined the soap, along with their profit. The old, familiar shame crept up into his belly.

But this time, a small, warm memory kept it from taking over. Emma believed in him. She had said it out loud, for all the world to hear.

"These things take time," Leah said. "You can't launch a successful side business overnight."

"That's true," Amanda said as she hitched up the apron. Because she was so petite, the fabric hung too low on her.

"Hey, what are you all doing in here without me?" Naomi asked as she barged into the kitchen. "I can hear you all talking from across the house. What's everyone worked up about this time?" Her eyes shifted to Amanda. "And why are you wearing my apron again? You're too short for it."

"Because I can't find mine. And the problem is that you're too tall, not that I'm too short."

Naomi flashed a mischievous grin. "Pretty sure the problem is always you, Amanda."

Amanda rolled her eyes.

"Anyway, what were you all talking about?" Naomi asked.

"How Miriam thinks I failed today," Benjamin said.

"That is absolutely not what I said."

"You didn't have to."

Miriam pinched the bridge of her nose. "I apologized. And I meant it. I'm sorry. Sometimes I just worry so much and…" She dropped her hand. "Never mind."

"It's *oll recht*. I know."

"Danki."

Benjamin knew that Miriam drove him crazy because she cared. It still drove him crazy, but it made it all right in the end. Most of the time.

"So how much did you end up selling today?" Amanda asked.

"Ach, vell..." Benjamin toed a crack in the worn linoleum floor.

"How much did you actually make?" Naomi asked.

Benjamin sighed. The moment had come that he had dreaded. "We didn't make anything. I think it might have cost more to make the soap then it sold for today."

Benjamin didn't want to look at Miriam, but when he did, the expression on her face was one of hurt. She was hurting for him and he knew it. But she quickly smoothed the expression and jumped into her usual protective mode. "Maybe this is a *gut* time to stop—"

"Then why did you say it went well?" Amanda interrupted.

Benjamin shrugged. "It just went well, that's all."

Amanda's eyes narrowed. "You mean things went well between you and Emma?" She glanced at Miriam, then back at Benjamin. "Ain't so?"

Benjamin shrugged again. "Maybe." He tried to look detached and nonchalant. He had never been either of those things. He could feel the smile tugging at the corner of his lips, tried to stop it, and couldn't.

"That's exactly what you meant," Amanda said. "I can see it all over your face."

"It doesn't have to be a bad thing," Leah said.

"We're not saying it's a bad thing," Miriam said.

"Just that it's not the best thing," Amanda finished for her.

"And we want the best for Benjamin," Miriam said.

"I know what's best for my own life."

"I'm not saying you don't."

Benjamin shot Miriam a look.

"It's just that sometimes, when emotions get the best of us, it's hard to see things clearly."

"I don't know why you're so worried all the time, Miriam."

"And I don't know why you're not worried all the time, Benji."

"Maybe emotions are getting the best of you right now, Miriam. You ever think of that? Maybe you're the one not seeing things clearly."

Miriam stiffened.

"Oll recht." Amanda put up a hand. "Maybe, since you didn't sell enough, this is a *gut* time to cut your losses and step away from it."

"You mean from Emma."

There was an awkward silence.

"Vell, ya," Amanda admitted after a moment. "Maybe the situation is working out for the best."

"Miriam wouldn't agree."

"I wouldn't agree with what?"

"You wouldn't want me to stop working with Emma."

"What?" Miriam looked confused.

"You're the one who always says I need help with stuff, right? You're the one who always wants to treat me like I'm still a *youngie*, ain't so?"

Miriam sputtered, but no discernible words came out.

Benjamin gave a decisive nod. "*Gut.* It's decided. Emma will keep helping me."

"Benjamin, you're not being fair," Miriam said. "You're twisting things around."

"I'm having fun with you, Miriam. Even though it's like pulling teeth to get you to see the joke."

"It wasn't very funny."

"I thought it was." Benjamin managed a weak smile, then he sighed and leaned against the wall. He hadn't realized how tired he was. "Emma and I are a team now. She has *gut* ideas and we're going to make a profit. Today was more of a focus on marketing. Next time, we'll sell better."

Miriam didn't respond for a moment. Her finger tapped slowly against the butcher-block countertop. "What do you mean by *team*?" she asked.

Benjamin shrugged. "I don't know. I guess we'll all just have to see."

Chapter Eleven

Emma was thankful that the next day was a visiting Sunday, so she didn't have to see everyone at a church meeting. Church Sundays had been hard for her ever since she started showing. She felt like she was on display with her enormous belly and her single status—as if she were a warning that everyone needed to heed. A few people in the district still clucked their tongues when they saw her, although most were more subtle about it, especially since the bishop was her uncle and he always stood up for her.

Emma managed to get through the day with some polite conversation. She was glad to see Mary and Sadie when they dropped by with their families, but the interaction left her drained and raw. She could not help but feel alone when surrounded by happy couples. As they all chatted and nibbled on pumpkin pie, Emma's gaze kept shifting to the window. In the distance, on the crest of the hill, she could see the fence that separated her from Stoneybrook Farm. Benjamin was on the other side. He had not come to visit. But why would he? They saw each other almost every weekday. And yet, she couldn't help but feel rejected.

Rejected by Benjamin Stoltzfus? Was she really worried about that? She would have laughed at the thought a few years ago. She had never seen him as a catch before.

But she had not understood how the world worked before. She had not grown up yet. She had not appreciated what really made a good man. Now she understood. And Benjamin wasn't just a good man, he was a good man for *her*. She didn't just see that logically. It wasn't a calculated observation because she needed a husband. She felt it deep down inside, in the spark of joy that zipped through her every time they were together.

But she was just a friend to him. A best friend. But a friend, nonetheless. He would not come visit her today. It was silly of her to want him to.

The next day, it was hard to put one foot in front of the other to march over to Stoneybrook Farm. The feeling of rejection weighed Emma down, tugging her back toward her house, whispering at her to give up, go back inside, and hide under the quilt. She had never been rejected before Liam came along. Amish boys had always wanted to court her and *Englisch* boys had wanted to date her during *Rumspringa*. They all said she was pretty, fun to be around, full of life. She had never known what it was to be lonely, and now she didn't know how to handle it.

Of course, there were lots of people who supported her—Sadie, Mary, Amos and Edna, even Eliza and Viola. But knowing that no one wanted to father her child, that no upright Amish man wanted to court her now… It was a pain that sat beneath her breastbone, sometimes dull and sometimes sharp, but always there.

"*Vell*, a friend is better than nothing," she said out loud to remind herself. "You're fortunate to have that, now." She clenched her fists and swung her arms as she heaved herself up the hill. The baby shifted inside and she smiled. "We have each other now and we always will. No one can take that away from us."

A loud honking broke the still afternoon air.

"Hey!" Benjamin shouted from the other side of the hill. "Be careful!" Something hissed, then honked in response.

Emma picked up her pace, even though she felt like a duck waddling up the incline. Her breath was coming fast by the time she crested the top of the hill and let herself through the gate.

"Watch out!" Benjamin shouted.

Emma froze. A white goose tore across the

muddy farmyard, head thrust forward on its long, snaky neck. Black eyes glittered like angry diamonds.

"Stop!" Benjamin shouted and sprinted after it. "Don't let her bite you!"

But the goose slowed down as she approached Emma, sized her up with those dark, accusatory eyes, and stopped hissing. The bird toddled closer, then stopped. They stared at one another for a long, hard moment. Emma slowly lowered herself into a crouch. "Hey there," she murmured.

Benjamin caught up and sputtered to a stop. "We got a guard goose."

"I can see that."

"I'm sorry she scared you."

"It's *oll recht*. She didn't scare me." Emma smiled. "*Vell*, just a little bit, maybe."

"I think she likes you." Benjamin shook his head. "Which doesn't make sense. You know how geese are." He handed Emma a paper cup full of grain. "Here, feed her some of this. That will seal the deal. She needs to know you're a friend." He grinned. "Although she seems to have figured that out on her own."

Emma took the cup and eased her hand toward the goose. It took all her willpower to keep her arm outstretched as she waited for the animal to bite. But instead, the goose extended her long neck and dived into the cup. Grain flew out as she rooted around, then raised her head to swallow everything in two big gulps. She thrust her head back into the cup, and a moment later the cup was empty. The goose waddled in a circle, plucking up the spilled grain from the dirt and swallowing it down. After she had picked the ground clean, she waddled back to the barn and paced in front of the goat pen.

"She'll let you come over without a problem now," Benjamin said.

"I hope so." Emma started to stand before she realized that was going to be harder than she had anticipated. But Benjamin was already there, his big, calloused hands closing around her arms and pulling her up. He made sure she was steady on her feet before letting go. *"Danki,"* Emma whispered as a surge of emotion came over her. It felt so good to be looked after by a man who cared about her.

As a friend, Emma reminded herself. She needed to stop thinking this way. "So, how did you end up with a guard goose?"

"Right, that." Benjamin chuckled. "Eliza and Gabriel King bought her to guard their chickens, but she kept chasing their daughter, Priss, so I volunteered to take her. They dropped her by yesterday. It ended up being quite a dramatic day. And she's still nipping and hissing at everything that comes near. I haven't been able to leave the property for fear she'll bite someone."

"That's a lot to take on."

"I couldn't let anything happen to her. She's a good girl. But, she's just, *vell*...a goose."

Emma laughed. Some of the rejection lifted. Benjamin hadn't come by on visiting Sunday because he'd been busy with a goose. It was a ridiculous reason, but sounded just like him.

"I can't believe she didn't attack you."

Emma smiled. "She has *gut* taste."

"She does." His tone was serious and thoughtful. "I think she's got an instinct for who's *gut* and who's bad." He cleared his throat and looked away.

"Do you really mean that? You don't think..." Emma couldn't say the words. She had already said too much.

Benjamin looked back at her. His gaze stayed steady and strong. "I don't think you're bad, Emma, if that's what you're asking."

Emma flinched at his directness, even though that was exactly what she had wanted to hear. "*Ya*. That's what I was asking."

Benjamin pulled off his straw hat and scratched his head. "Why is everyone always so quick to condemn women in your situation? Men are equally guilty for these things, but no one treats them the same way when they get caught. That says a lot, if you ask me."

Emma stood staring at him. She had no idea how to respond to that. All she knew was that she wanted to throw herself into his arms and thank him for being exactly who he was. She swallowed and managed to ask, "Do you really mean that?"

"Of course I do." His expression hardened. "It makes me angry, when I think of how people in our church district, and your district back in Holmes County, judge you. But those same people don't pay as much attention to actions that hurt another person, especially when it's hurting a person who can't speak up for themselves. As if *that* doesn't matter, but what you did does. It's easy for them to point fingers at you, while ignoring other sins around them." His face shifted and he allowed a small smile. He never kept an angry look for long. "But let's not think about them. I'm glad you came back today. I wasn't sure you would."

Emma's brow creased. "Why not?"

Benjamin shrugged. "After I messed everything up at the farmers market, I was worried you might give up on me."

"*Me*, give up on *you*?"

Benjamin looked sheepish. *"Ya."*

"I'm the one who's the problem, not—"

"Nee," Benjamin cut her off. He raised his eyebrows. "Didn't I just say something about that?"

Emma laughed. Suddenly she felt so light-hearted and free that she wanted to sing. *"Ya.* You did."

"Oll recht, then."

She enjoyed the rest of the day with Benjamin. They calculated their earnings—or losses, rather—and recorded it all in the accounting book. He sighed when she told him the exact numbers, but then he just shrugged and said, *"Vell,* we best get back to work, then." Benjamin always recovered quickly. That was one thing that Emma had always liked about him. It was impossible to quench his enthusiasm.

They started over with a new batch of soap, measuring, boiling, and stirring—and laughing all the time. As well as occasionally avoiding the guard goose, who circled them with accusatory eyes if they dared to get too close to the territory that she had claimed.

As the sun lowered and long, evening shadows stretched their fingers across the fields, Benjamin set down a plastic soap mold and stood up from his stool. "I have to bring the goats in from the south pasture. Want to come with me?"

Emma was surprised at how much the simple invitation meant. "Sure."

The guard goose waddled after them, then stopped when she reached the edge of the farm-yard. She made a beeline for a crow sitting on a fence post and hissed at the invader. The crow flapped its wings, rose into the sky, and flew away. The goose looked satisfied as she went back to riffling through the grass with her bright orange bill.

"She needs a name," Emma said as they headed into a muddy field.

"Belinda," Benjamin said.

Emma laughed. "That was fast. What made you think of it?"

Benjamin shrugged. "Just seems right, ain't so?"

"*Ya*. It does sound like a *gut* name for a goose."

"*Oll recht*. That's settled."

Emma liked strolling across the farm with Benjamin as the sky faded to purple and the last rays of sunlight outlined the rolling hills in a golden glow. Benjamin took her elbow when they tramped across the two-by-fours laid over the rocky creek that gave Stoneybrook Farm its name. The loose boards rocked beneath their weight. "Careful, it's not much of a bridge," Benjamin warned. Emma had not thought to be afraid, not when he was guiding her across.

When they reached the south pasture, most of the grass was nibbled down to stubs. Goats bleated as they grazed, while two kids leaped and chased one another. "Don't get too close," Benjamin said. "They're friendly but I don't want to risk one knocking you down. You know how goats can be. Got to protect that little *boppli*, ain't so?"

Emma hung back as he rounded up the goats. She liked that he had mentioned the baby directly. Somehow, they had gotten past the awkwardness of the situation. Benjamin was treating her like he would anyone else. He wasn't avoiding what was happening, but he wasn't making a big deal of it, either. That felt just right to her.

She watched him stop to pat the goats and call each one by name. He scratched a goat behind the ears and murmured something to her. The goat nudged him and flicked her tail. Ollie appeared, circled behind the herd, and barked. Emma followed Benjamin and the animals across the pastureland as she pondered what he had said earlier that afternoon. He didn't think that she was bad. He didn't condemn her.

Maybe, just maybe, she could indulge the feelings for him that were building inside her. Maybe he could feel the same way about her too. Her hand went instinctively to her belly as she surveyed the farmland spread in front of her. The rolling, green hills, the split rail fences and weathered outbuildings, the old rambling farmhouse with its double porch and tin roof. She could be happy here. She could have a life here, belong here.

There was a bang as the screen door to the farmhouse slammed shut. In the evening shadows, Emma could make out the silhouette of a woman slip into the backyard and empty a bucket of dirty water. A chicken clucked and dodged the splash as the water splattered the dirt. Belinda honked in the distance and a goat bleated. A propane lamp clicked on inside the farmhouse, and the yellow light poured through the window, illuminating the woman. It was Miriam. She stretched her back before turning and walking back into the house, the screen door slamming behind her again.

Emma sighed. The hope felt farther away now. She could never belong here. Not fully. She should never let herself forget that. Otherwise, the disappointment would be too much to bear.

Emma went through the motions of life, trying to hang on to hope, savoring the fun she and Benjamin had together. Each hour with him was like a little escape from reality. But reality was coming, and she couldn't pretend that it wasn't. For now, her baby was tucked away, safe and sound inside her. But soon, that baby would be in her arms, needing the loving family that every child deserved. She hoped that she could be enough. All she wanted was to be a good mother. But no matter how much she filled in the gap for a father, that gap would be there. She could not be everything at all times.

Her hope slipped a little more when the youth group arrived at the Yoder farm for a singing. Amos encouraged her to stay and sing, but when the buggies began arriving with smiling, laughing *youngies*, she could not bear it. Some were the same age as her. But their lives seemed so carefree and simple in comparison. The girls would chat and giggle together and act coy when the boys complimented them. Then they would pair off and the boys would drive the girls home in their courting buggies beneath the stars and moonlight, alongside the quiet, sleeping fields.

That romance was impossible for her now. Emma would never know the thrill of being asked to ride home in a young man's buggy again. The joy of being chosen, of being noticed and valued. Of feeling pretty. The excitement of possibilities waiting to unfold.

So she slipped away as the buggies gathered and the girls set out their casserole dishes and pie tins on the folding tables in the barn. She could see the scene lit up by the propane lamps through the open double doors. The girls stood shyly by the tables as the boys congregated nearby, working up the courage to talk to them. The Yoders' buggy horse whinnied from his stall. A rooster crowed and wind swept bright red leaves from the maple tree that stood beside the barn.

Emma had seen enough. She began to walk away, into the darkness beyond the farmyard.

"Are you leaving?"

Emma turned to see Edna following her. She looked plump and matronly with her generous midsection and starched apron. Emma had a sudden urge to hug her. She needed mothering right now, but needed to be a mother herself, instead. So she swallowed hard and resisted. But Edna must have sensed her need. She stepped forward and pulled Emma into a hug. "Even mothers need mothering sometimes."

"How did you know?" Emma asked as she rested her chin on Edna's soft shoulder.

"It isn't hard to see."

When Emma pulled away from the hug, Edna's eyes were moist. "*Kumme* in and sing with us. It's going to be a pleasant evening."

Emma sighed and looked down at her hands. "I don't belong with them anymore. The only reason I'm here is because you and Amos are hosting. Otherwise, I wouldn't be included."

Edna hesitated, then nodded. "I understand. But if you change your mind, *vell*, you know how long these things last."

"*Danki.*" Emma knew they would be singing

for two hours or so, then they would mingle and eat for a while before pairing off into the courting buggies to go home. She appreciated Edna's offer, but she planned to stay outside until it was over. Or else hide in her room. But that felt too lonely. At least if she walked beneath the stars, she could feel connected to something bigger than herself. She could remember that a God big enough to create that vast universe was watching over her and her unborn baby.

She hurried around the side of the house before any of the *youngies* noticed her. As she reached the kitchen garden, she heard footsteps up the hill and turned to see a dark silhouette moving toward her. She recognized that walk, even though she couldn't make out the face. "Hey, Benji," she said.

He loped the last few yards down the hill. "Hey, Emma."

"I wondered when you were going to show up for the singing. They're already in the barn. But I don't think they've started yet."

Benjamin hesitated. "I, uh, didn't *kumme* for the singing."

"You didn't?"

"I thought you might be feeling left out."

"You came here…to see me?"

He shrugged and smiled. "I came to take you

away for the evening. Go somewhere we belong."

"But you do belong here." She nodded behind
her, toward the barn.

"*Ach*, not really. Ever seen me try to play volleyball with them? Or keep up with them at a
barn raising?"

"People like you, Benji."

"Maybe. But the boys in there don't have a lot
of respect for me. I'm no *gut* at the things that
earn their respect."

Emma wanted to argue, but she knew it was
true. "There are more important things."

"Like what?"

"Kindness, gentleness, self-control. Those are
the things that should earn a man respect."

Benjamin grunted. "That's not how it works."

"*Vell*, it should. If we lived by what we claim
to believe."

Benjamin was silent for a moment. "I appreciate that, Emma."

"It's true. I wouldn't have said it otherwise."

Benjamin flashed a playful grin and nudged
her with his elbow. "So, you want to get out of
here?"

Emma laughed. She knew this was one of her
last chances for any spontaneity. Everything
would be different soon. It would be good to
have her precious baby in her arms, but it would

change how she lived her life. She was just about to give Benjamin an enthusiastic yes when he cleared his throat and added, "Just as friends, of course. I figure we earned it after all the work we've done together. We can think of it as a business lunch...for dinner."

"Oh." Emma wasn't sure how to feel. She had been excited until he pointed out that it would just be as friends. She should have known that was coming. Emma had let her emotions fool her into believing that something more might be developing between them. Benjamin hesitated again. "We don't have to. Just thought you'd like to get away, that's all. You know, like we used to. Remember when we used to just take off together?"

"Ya." Emma warmed at the memory. They had always been one another's escape. And now, here he was, rescuing her again. Only as a friend, but what else could she expect? "We're too old to sneak down to the pond to go swimming, then eat sandwiches on the banks. Where do you want to go?"

"Remember where my parents used to take us to celebrate after we sheared the Angoras and sold the wool each year?"

"My favorite restaurant in the world, the Old Amish Kitchen."

"Want to go back there?" He added quickly, "Like I said, just as friends."

Emma cringed a little. He didn't have to keep reiterating that. But she appreciated his honesty. Better to make things clear. It was kinder that way. Benjamin was too thoughtful to let her get her hopes up. She knew that she needed to agree in order to save face. It would be humiliating if he suspected that she hoped for something more. "*Ya.* Of course. As friends." She said the words a little too forcefully to make sure he believed her, even as her heart wanted to say the opposite. "Just let me tell Edna I'm going out so she doesn't worry."

Twenty minutes later, Benjamin's buggy rolled to a stop in the parking lot of the Old Amish Kitchen. Clyde tugged at the bit, shook his head, and lowered his muzzle to a strip of grass just beyond the pavement. Benjamin had taken the last spot designated for buggies. He had not realized the place would be packed with people from the church district. He didn't want Emma to feel uncomfortable.

"It's awfully crowded." He turned to look at her. "We can go somewhere else."

She hesitated. "I've been craving their apple strudel for ages." Then she swallowed hard and he saw the flicker of vulnerability pass over her face before she added, "But…"

"I can go in and get it to go." The more he thought about it, the more he realized what a foolish thing he'd done by coming here. He had been so set on making Emma feel better that he hadn't thought about the consequences. Someone was sure to see them. If that happened, talk would spread as fast as a wildfire through a cornfield during a drought. He wasn't embarrassed to be seen with Emma. Absolutely not. But he was worried about what it would cost her if there was gossip about her being out with a man. Not to mention what his sisters would have to say.

Benjamin studied the cheerful, yellow building with exposed wooden beams, turquoise shutters, and window boxes filled with pink tulips. He wondered if they were plastic, this time of year. They were pretty either way. The scene was something out of a whimsical German fairy tale, especially with the big wooden windmill in the yard beside the building, painted yellow and turquoise to match. The blades turned slowly in the crisp, autumn breeze. Coming here as a child, it had felt like a magical place, something out of a storybook—one that included Black Forest cake and chicken schnitzel. Back then, life had been simple and straightforward.

Nothing felt simple or straightforward anymore. Especially since he had messed up yet again. He should have remembered how busy this place could get. He had taken enough of a risk just by asking Emma here. She could have mistaken it as an invitation to be courted. They had rekindled their friendship, but she was still out of his league. Besides, he wanted to give her an escape for the night, not create an awkward situation. He would never put that pressure on her.

"It's really crowded," Emma said as she shrank back in her seat. "That might not be a bad idea, if you don't mind going in for it."

"Of course I don't mind."

"All I want is apple strudel."

"You sure?"

"*Ya.* It's already made, so it will be quick."

"*Oll recht.*" Benjamin hopped down from the seat. "Sounds *gut.*" He remembered how they used to stare at the bakery case when they were children, hands and noses pressed against the glass. In the end, Emma always chose the apple strudel.

He gave Clyde a quick pat on the neck before tying the reins to the hitching post and hurrying into the restaurant. As he opened the door, murmuring voices and clinking china welcomed him along with the aroma of freshly baked bread.

The place was packed and he whispered a quick prayer of thanks that he had not brought Emma inside. An Amish hostess wearing a white *kapp* and blue cape dress looked up from her station. "It's going to be a twenty-or-thirty-minute wait, is that *oll recht*?"

"I'm just getting dessert from the bakery case."

"Perfect. You can go straight to the register at the counter."

She looked tired and thin and Benjamin wondered if Emma would be faced with a future where she had to work long hours on her feet, just to make ends meet as a single mother. His heart ached at the thought. How could any man abandon her and their child? He simply could not understand it.

As Benjamin cut through the crowd to the bakery case, he wondered what had happened between Emma and the father of her baby. He had not thought too much about it. It wasn't his business. But whatever had happened, Emma was clearly hurt by it—how couldn't she be?

"What can I get you?" the Amish woman behind the counter asked.

"Oh. Right. I'll take the apple strudel. Two of them. And can you make one of them a really big slice, please?"

"For certain sure." The woman slid open the glass case. "Will that be all?"

Benjamin glanced at the menu written in chalk above the bakery case. Emma had always liked their lemonade. Maybe she still did. "I'll take two lemonades, please. The raspberry vanilla ones."

"Oll recht."

A few minutes later, Benjamin was carrying a white bakery box while he balanced a cardboard tray with two lemonades in his other hand. The lemonade had been a bad idea. He would have to make sure not to drop it. But he had managed to get in and out of there without anyone seeing him. That was certainly a victory. He let out a big sigh of relief, readjusted the tray, and was trying to push open the door with his elbow when he heard a voice behind him. "Got your hands full?"

Benjamin froze. He knew that voice. Viola Esch. Of all people.

She hobbled over just as an *Englischer* pulled open the door from the outside. The man held it open and nodded to Benjamin and Viola as they filed into the parking lot. Benjamin's mind started spinning. He needed to think fast.

"Two of everything, huh?"

"Uh. *Ya.*"

"I know you're a big eater, but you didn't get two drinks just for yourself."

Benjamin flinched. The lemonade had given him away. "*Ya. Vell*, it's been *gut* to see you,

Viola. Hope you're doing *gut*. Take care." He turned toward his buggy and held his breath. Maybe she wouldn't follow. But he heard the tap, tap, tap of her cane behind him.

"No need to walk so fast, young man."

Benjamin sighed and slowed his pace. He was caught for certain sure. He didn't mind what people said about him, but he wanted to protect Emma's privacy. They were here just as friends, but Viola might not report it quite like that.

"Ah." Viola pointed toward his buggy with her cane. "I see there's someone there. She squinted through her bifocals. "Can't quite make out who, yet." She looked at Benjamin and raised her eyebrows. "Did you take my advice?"

He gulped and tightened his grip on the cardboard bakery box. His palms were starting to sweat. *"Nee."*

A car's headlights swept through the parking lot, illuminating the front bench seat of Benjamin's buggy. Emma's profile became clear in the yellow glow, before dropping her into shadow again.

"Ah! You did. Now why did you lie to me just now?"

"I didn't, it's not like that—"

"We won't worry about it. What matters is that you're courting her now. It's about time."

"Nee, we're not courting."

Viola shot him a look. "You're both out together, in a buggy, getting dinner."

"It's just dessert."

Viola rolled her eyes.

"So have you proposed yet?" She kept hobbling toward the buggy and Benjamin stumbled over his feet as he tried to keep up while balancing the two foam cups of lemonade in the cardboard to-go tray.

"Proposed? Viola! I told you, we're not even courting."

"It's *oll recht*, dear." She patted his arm. "I know how you *youngies* like to keep these things quiet until just a few weeks before the wedding." She winked at him. "They'll be a big announcement soon, I'm sure. You don't have time to wait, ain't so?"

That was the one thing that Viola was right about. Emma didn't have long until the baby came. Benjamin's jaw tightened. He wished there was more he could do for her.

They reached the buggy and Viola rapped on the side with her cane. Emma jumped and looked over. Her face fell. "Oh. Viola."

"So. Let's cut to the chase. When's the wedding? Benjamin won't give me a straight answer."

The color drained from Emma's face. "What…?" Her eyes cut to Benjamin.

He shook his head. "Viola, I told you, we're not even courting."

Viola nodded toward the food and drinks in Benjamin's hands. "Just out for the evening, together. With no one else."

"Exactly."

Viola snorted.

Benjamin felt hot. His pulse tapped against his temple. Emma would be humiliated when word got out. "Listen, Emma and I are friends. Only friends. We've only ever been friends and we will only ever be friends. *Oll recht?*"

Viola narrowed her eyes and adjusted her glasses. *"Vell."*

"I'm sorry. I didn't mean for that to come out so heated."

"You ever heard of that famous *Englischer* man who used to write plays?"

"What?" Benjamin shook his head.

"That man from way back. What do the *Englischers* call him?" She frowned. "Shakespeare. That's right."

"Uh, I think I might have heard of him." Amish school only went through eighth grade and it didn't cover worldly *Englisch* literature, but the name was vaguely familiar.

"I used to teach school." Viola waved her hand in a dismissive gesture. "It was a long time ago. I got into the habit of reading. And once you start it's hard to stop. Call it my little rebellion." She gave Emma a pointed look. "We all have a rebellious phase, dear. One way or another."

Benjamin stepped between Viola and Emma. "So, this Shakespeare fellow…"

"Ah, right. He wrote 'the lady doth protest too much.' That's a fancy way of saying that the lady is trying too hard to claim that something isn't true." She raised an eyebrow. "Or, in this case, the gentleman."

There were a few beats of silence. "Viola, is this your way of saying that you don't believe me?"

Viola smiled like a cat who had had gotten into the cream. "That's exactly what I'm saying."

Chapter Twelve

Benjamin knew he was in for it. And he was. It took exactly twelve hours and twenty-one minutes for word to spread to his sisters. Amanda went to Bluebird Hills Feed and Seed the next morning and came back with a lot more than vitamins to supplement the goats' diet. She came back with news of Benjamin's impending marriage. Amanda told Naomi, who happened to be the first person that Amanda saw as soon as she could leap from the still-moving buggy, stumble to the ground as it rolled to a stop, and get the words out. They both marched straight to the kitchen, where Miriam was rolling out a piecrust.

Benjamin heard the raised voices through the open kitchen window, since the noise drifted all the way to the milking shed, where he sat hunched over the diesel-powered milking machine, disinfecting it with a rag soaked in cleaner. The chemical smell burned his eyes, but he liked the lemon scent. He enjoyed the feel of everything being clean and new, so he didn't mind the fumes.

Benjamin threw down the rag and stood up as soon as he heard footsteps pounding toward him. He could see the three of them through the window. They barreled across the farmyard like a small army, arms pumping, jaws clenched, eyes sparking. *Well, that didn't take long,* Benjamin thought. They passed out of sight, around the corner of the building, and then the door swung open. It slammed against the wooden wall and made the building rattle.

"Benjamin!" Miriam shouted. "Are you in here?"

He sighed and turned to face them. "Yep. Finished the milking and was just cleaning up—"

"That doesn't matter right now."

Benjamin sighed again.

"You're marrying her?" Amanda asked. Her face jutted forward as she stuck her hands on her hips.

"How could you, Benjamin?" Naomi asked. "You didn't even tell us you were courting!"

"*Vell*, we all saw it, clear as day," Miriam said. "We just didn't want to believe it."

There was a series of thuds outside before Leah swept into the milking shed, breathing hard. "Benjamin, you're getting married?"

"*Nee.*"

"I could hear you all clear across the farm-yard." She shook her head, the hurt flashing in her eyes. "Why did you keep it from me? We're twins. We don't have secrets." Her face crumpled. "Or I thought we didn't."

"I'm not keeping any secrets from you."

"Planning on getting married is a secret, certain sure," Amanda said.

"I am not planning on getting married."

"*Vell*, that's not what Sarah over at the Feed and Seed said. And she heard it from Lizzy Peachy, who heard it straight from Viola Esch."

Benjamin shot Amanda a look. "Viola Esch. Really? She's your source of ultimate truth now?"

"She has a way of knowing what's what, Benji," Amanda said.

Miriam held up her hand. "*Oll recht.* Everyone calm down and let's get to the bottom of this." She stared Benjamin down in a way that only a mother or a big sister can. "Amanda has a point. Where there's smoke there's fire."

"Not here. I told Viola that Emma and I are friends. Only friends."

"Then where did she get the idea?"

Benjamin scratched the back of his neck. "Uh, *vell*, I might have gone out to the Old Amish Kitchen with Emma last night. And I might have run into Viola."

Miriam threw up her hands. "You may as well have sent out wedding invitations, like the *Englischers* do."

"It was just two friends, going out. Casually."

"Alone. In a buggy. For dinner." Miriam's eyebrows rose higher with each word.

"That's what Viola said," Benjamin muttered. "And it wasn't dinner. It was only dessert."

"I'll be sure to let all the witnesses know that little detail."

"Come on, Miriam. Emma needs a friend. I had to cheer her up last night. It's what friends do. You don't need to make such a big deal about it."

"You can be her friend in a reasonable way. But going out like that? What were you thinking?"

"Exactly what I told you. That she needed a friend. So, I took her to her favorite restaurant."

"You took her there. See how much that sounds like you're courting her?"

Benjamin frowned. "When you put it that way. If you twist it all around to make it sound like it." He clenched his jaw and tried to put his thoughts together. A goat bleated from the pen, followed by Belinda's honking. "You know what, I don't like the way you're coming at this. So what if we were courting? What would be so bad about that? She's a *gut* woman and I'd be blessed to marry her."

"So you admit it." Amanda leaned closer. "You *are* courting."

"*Nee*. But I wish we were."

Silence filled the room.

"He's right," Leah said after a long, tense moment. "There's nothing wrong with them courting. We should just let it be."

"I told you we're not courting."

"There's nothing wrong with him wanting to court her," Leah corrected herself.

Miriam let out a sharp sigh. "We like Emma."

"You've never liked Emma," Benjamin snapped.

"We just don't like her for you. As a *fraa* for you."

"She's always led you to trouble," Amanda said. "Ever since you two were *kinner*."

"And now she's in real trouble, Benjamin." Miriam's expression softened as she spoke. "I'm sorry. I know how much you care about her. But it's not your responsibility to get her out of this, Benjamin. She shouldn't expect that of you."

"She doesn't," Benjamin said. "She asks nothing of me. Nothing." He stood up straighter and stared Miriam down. "I want to help her. Can't you understand that? This is what *I* want."

Miriam hesitated before she spoke. Her eyes looked sad. "It's a lot to take on Benji. We were all hurt that you kept the engagement from us—"

"We're not even courting," Benjamin interrupted.

"*Oll recht.* We were hurt because we thought you kept the engagement from us."

"The imaginary engagement."

"*Ya.* But we're upset because whether or not you're engaged—or even courting—there's still something to it. It's clear to us how you feel about her, Benji. We're afraid that you don't see that a relationship with Emma would be too much to take on. She might not stay true to the faith. She's already jumped the fence once. And even if she keeps our ways, are you really ready to be a *daed*?"

Benjamin looked away. "*Vell*, you don't have to worry about it. She's not interested in me like that. We're only friends. And that's all we ever will be." The humiliation crept up his body, like cold, rising water. It hurt to admit that the woman he loved did not feel the same way. But Emma had been very quick to agree last night that they were going out as friends. Nothing more.

"Then it's best not to advertise a relationship. People will talk, Benji. It puts her in an awkward position. You could even be taking away her chances of finding a *daed* for her *boppli*, if everyone thinks she's already taken."

"Don't you think I know that?" He ran his

fingers through his hair so hard that it hurt his scalp. "That's why I was running in, alone, for takeout. Viola just happened to catch me."

"But if you hadn't put yourself in that position, she wouldn't have caught you."

"Emma deserves to get out. She shouldn't have to live like an outcast."

"We're not suggesting that she live like an outcast," Naomi said. "Amos and Edna are making sure she gets out. She was at the Hochstetlers' work frolic, ain't so?"

"We're just suggesting that you back away a little bit," Miriam said gently. "For her sake, as much as yours."

Benjamin shook his head and pushed past his sisters.

"Benjamin, wait!" Leah shouted after him.

But Benjamin didn't stop. He had had enough and he stormed outside without speaking another word. But he couldn't get away from what Miriam had said. Her words clanged inside his mind. What if she were right? What if the best thing that he could do for Emma were to leave her alone?

Emma wasn't sure how to feel when she showed up at Stoneybrook Farm that afternoon. The night before, she had felt special for the first time in what seemed like forever. Benja-

min had reminded her what it was like to be valued—as a friend, at least. She had almost been
able to pretend that it could become something
more as they drove alone in the buggy, beneath
the clear, bright stars, winding along the back
roads in the still, silent evening. But then she had
seen the look on Benjamin's face when Viola had
caught them together. He had been mortified. He
had fought hard to convince Viola that he and
Emma were friends and nothing more. Emma
had never seen him so determined. She didn't
hold it against him, of course. She understood.
But it still hurt. Now she was worried how they
would interact today. Would the easy camaraderie they had found be lost again?

She soon discovered the answer was yes. It
was clear as soon as they began popping the
soap from the molds and wrapping it in tissue
paper. Benjamin kept stumbling over his words
and glancing around, unable to meet her eyes.
There were long periods of silence, broken only
by the whisper of tissue paper and the snip-snap
of scissors cutting twine. Emma tried to focus
on the work, but all she could think about was
that Benjamin was embarrassed to be seen with
her. Well, of course he was.

The door creaked opened and Emma tensed.
Being rejected by Benjamin was bad enough.

Now she would have to see one of his sisters too. She just hoped it wasn't Miriam.

It was.

Miriam's lips tightened when she walked into the room and saw Emma hunched over the folding table. Miriam nodded, then managed a polite, "Hello." But Emma could hear the reluctance in her tone.

"Hello," Emma said. "How are you?"

Miriam sighed. "Fine. We're all fine." She bent down, hefted a heavy sack from a pile in the corner, and balanced it on her shoulder.

"Here." Benjamin scooted his chair back from the table. "Let me get that."

"Nonsense," Miriam said. "I've got it."

"You sure?"

"How long have I been working this farm, Benji?" Miriam gave a little smile as she hustled out of the room, her compact body looking too small to manage the load.

"And how long have I been asking if you need help?" Benjamin shouted after her.

"Your *schweschder* sure is tough," Emma said.

"Too tough, sometimes," Benjamin said. He broke the tension with a smile. "I'm just joking. I mean, she *is* tough as nails, but I admire her for that. She's had to be."

"*Ya.* I can see that. But…" Emma let the sentence fade out, afraid that she might say too much.

Benjamin glanced over at her. "I know what you're wondering and, *ya*, it's true. She's not always easy to live with."

"Oh. I didn't mean to suggest..." Emma wasn't sure what to say. She didn't want to come between Benjamin and his sister.

"It's *oll recht*. We have a saying around here. 'Miriam knows best.'" He gave a conspiratorial wink. "Just don't tell her I told you."

"You don't have to worry about that." Emma tried to smile, but it came out as more of a grimace.

Benjamin frowned when he saw her expression. "It isn't you."

"What do you mean?"

"The reason that Miriam is acting distant and aloof. Part of it is just her way. Part of it is..." He shifted in his seat. "*Vell*, she worries too much. She always sees the bad that can happen, instead of the *gut*."

"I'm the bad that can happen, ain't so?" The words flew out of her mouth before she could stop them. She had been holding too much inside for too long.

Benjamin sucked his breath in through his teeth. "*Ach, nee.*" He shook his head. "I'm sorry, Emma. I said the wrong thing. I didn't mean—"

"I know you didn't mean to hurt me, but you

can't get around the facts. Miriam thinks I'm a bad influence."

Benjamin opened his mouth, then closed it again. He turned his focus to the twine that he was tying around a bar of soap. "I don't know what to say, Emma. I don't want to hurt you."

"It's *oll recht*. We've always been honest with each other. Besides, you don't need to say anything. I can see how Miriam feels, certain sure."

"She's wrong, Emma. One hundred percent wrong."

Emma set down the plastic mold in her hand and met Benjamin's eyes. "Do you really mean that?"

"Of course I do."

Emma breathed in and let it out slowly. She could see that he was telling the truth. But that hadn't stopped him from trying to hide any evidence of a relationship with her from the community last night. She nodded, unsure of how to respond. It was too confusing. So instead, she reached for the bar of soap in his hand. "Here. Let me tie the twine."

Her fingers brushed over his, sending a flurry of emotions cascading through her. His touch was so safe and familiar—yet it also held a new excitement that she had never felt before. He let his hand linger on hers for a moment longer than necessary. Or was she imagining that? Either way, she was left flustered, with her heart beating harder than it should.

Benjamin turned his attention to the wrapped bars of soap. His cheeks were splotched with red and Emma wondered if he, too, felt as flustered as she had by the touch. No, it was probably embarrassment over needing help. "Sorry, I'm no *gut* at that," he said. "Never could get a bow to look right."

So, it *was* just embarrassment, then. Emma gave him an encouraging smile even as her stomach sank. "There are more important things than being able to tie a pretty bow."

"You know, Emma, I'm not *gut* at saying how I feel, but—"

A loud honk interrupted him. Belinda stormed past the door that Miriam had left open and waddled across the room.

"No intruders in here," Benjamin said to her. "You can relax."

The goose scanned the room with black, beady eyes until she seemed satisfied, honked one more time for good measure, then waddled back out the door.

Benjamin chuckled. "She's very serious about protecting her territory."

Emma laughed, but her heart wasn't in it. She wanted to know what Benjamin had been about to say, but the moment was lost.

* * *

The next day, Edna hosted a work party to prepare for Emma's baby. A tight knot formed in her belly at the thought of all those women coming over to openly acknowledge a situation that still felt shameful. She was not sorry that she was having this baby. Ever since she learned that she was expecting, Emma had felt a deep love—a need, even—for this unborn child. But she was sorry for the way it was happening. In a perfect world, she would have this baby *and* a husband—but a better husband than Liam would have been. A husband like Benjamin.

Emma frowned. Wishful thinking wasn't helpful. There would be no perfect, happy ending for her. She would have the baby she loved and that would be enough, because it had to be. It would just be a little family of two. Two wasn't so bad, was it? No, it wasn't. But she could not stop herself from wanting more.

"Get on now, Amos," Edna said as she made a shooing motion.

Emma's attention jerked back to her surroundings. Was it already time for them to arrive?

"The women will be here soon," Edna said.

Amos winked at Emma. "I know where I don't belong. Best go on down to the orchard and check on how the pears are doing."

Emma wished he could stay. She always felt

better when Amos was around. But he couldn't participate in a sewing circle, of course. She watched as he grabbed his straw hat from the peg on the wall, shoved it onto his head, and walked out the door whistling a tune from the *Ausbund*.

The buggies began arriving as soon as he left. Not surprisingly, Viola was the first in the door. As usual, she did not wait for anyone to answer her knock, but let herself in with a loud, "Hello," and hobbled straight to the couch. Mary and Becky filed in soon after, followed by Sadie and her sister-in-law, Arleta. Katie Miller and Eliza strode in last. A blast of cold autumn air swept in with them.

"What a *gut* surprise," Edna said as she ushered them in. "I figured one of you would have to stay at the store." Katie and her husband, Levi, owned Aunt Fannie's Amish Gift Shop and Eliza and her husband, Gabriel, both worked for them.

"Gabriel is filling in for us," Katie said as they settled into one of the folding chairs Edna had put beside the black potbellied stove, since the couch and wicker rocker could not seat everyone. The room was full, but the mood felt cozy instead of crowded. Emma could almost relax, if she forgot what they were all there to do.

"I love the wooden baby rattles I bought at the shop," Sadie said. "They're just perfect." She smiled and her entire face beamed with joy. "I laid them out in our nursery so I can look at them and daydream about what's coming."

Emma wondered what it would be like to have a house of her own, with a husband to love her and father her baby. She imagined sitting in a rocker in a nursery, her newborn in her arms, Benjamin standing beside— Emma shook her head. Benjamin again. This had to stop.

"What is it?" Eliza asked. "You don't like the toys you bought for the *boppli*?"

"Huh?"

"You just shook your head."

"*Ach, nee.* I was thinking about something."

"About what?" Eliza pushed her glasses up her nose and stared at Emma, waiting for an answer.

"Nothing important."

"How about some pumpkin spice cake?" Edna asked.

Emma gave her a grateful look and Edna responded with a barely perceptible nod as she removed the lid from the cake tin on the coffee table. She began passing out slices when there was a knock on the front door. Emma stiffened. She had hoped that no one else would show up.

"Come in!" Edna shouted as she handed Viola an extra-large slice topped with a generous layer of cream cheese frosting.

The door creaked open in the entry hall, followed by rustling, then footsteps, and all of the Stoltzfus sisters appeared in the threshold of the living room. Suddenly the room went from cozy to crowded.

"Sorry we're late," Leah said. "We had to finish our chores before we could come over." She looked over at Emma and her grin seemed genuine. "It's *gut* to see you. I'm always so busy I haven't had a chance to visit when you've come over to work with Benjamin."

"I know how it is on a farm," Emma said.

Miriam, Amanda, and Naomi said a quick hello to the room without acknowledging Emma specifically. Miriam's face stayed as tight as ever. Amanda and Naomi smiled, but it didn't reach their eyes. An awkward silence descended. The scrape of metal forks against porcelain was the only sound.

"*Gut* thing I put out extra folding chairs," Edna said as she motioned for them to have a seat. "*Danki* for coming, everyone. This is a great turnout."

Emma wondered if everyone could feel the tension. Maybe she was imagining it because she was so afraid of their rejection.

"We've got a variety of projects to finish." Edna pointed to the coffee table, which was covered in baskets filled with fabric and sewing supplies. "Everything's here. A lot of the projects are partially finished, but Emma and I can't get them all done in time."

"Not much time left," Viola said.

Emma's hand moved to her belly. *"Nee,"* she murmured and looked down.

"I was glad to see that Benjamin took you out to the Old Amish Kitchen," Viola said. "Now that he's courting you—"

"We told you we're not courting," Emma interrupted. At the exact same time, Sadie exclaimed, "That's *wunderbar!*" Mary gasped and murmured, "I'm so happy for you both." And Katie Miller laughed and said, "I'm always the last to hear anything." Becky reached over, patted Emma's knee, and said, "He's cute!"

While everyone spoke at once, Miriam said something, but no one heard over the excited chatter. Emma watched with a sinking heart as Miriam looked around the room with her jaw clenched. When no one stopped to listen to her, she stood up. Even though she was small and compact, she had a big presence. "They are *not* courting." This time she had spoken loudly enough to get everyone's attention.

The happy chatter disappeared instantly. All eyes darted to Miriam. The room was so silent that they could hear the creak of Edna's wicker rocking chair.

Miriam cleared her throat. "I didn't mean to

shout. But no one was listening…" She stood awkwardly for a moment as everyone waited. "I just wanted you all to know that they are not courting. That's all." She smoothed her apron. "It's best if everyone knows the truth, instead of going on rumors."

"I saw them with my own eyes," Viola said. "That's not a rumor."

"And they told you they were just out as friends."

Viola raised an eyebrow. "And you believe that?"

"Of course I do," Miriam snapped. "Those two are *not* courting."

Emma flinched at Miriam's tone. She was pretty sure a few other women in the room did too.

Miriam took a deep breath and exhaled. "I'm sorry. That came out wrong. I just think it's best that we're all clear on what's going on, which is to say, nothing. Nothing is going on."

"I think we should ask Emma," Edna said. "She can tell us better than anyone." Edna gave Emma an encouraging nod.

"Miriam's right. Benjamin and I are friends. Just friends." Her face burned with shame under the weight of everyone's eyes. They were all staring at her, hanging on every word. "He made that very clear. I mean, we both did. We both agree. Friends and friends only. It's what's best for us."

Viola snorted. "Everyone here knows what's actually for the best." She narrowed her eyes at Miriam. "Except for one of us."

"They're adults," Miriam said. "They can decide for themselves."

"If you let them."

"I'm not standing in the way of anything."

Viola raised her eyebrows. "Then why were you so quick to claim they are not courting?"

"I think it's important to stop gossip."

"Time has a way of proving or disproving gossip," Viola said. "We'll just have to wait and see, ain't so?"

"Then there's no reason to keep talking about it," Edna said gently.

Amanda tugged at Miriam's apron. Miriam looked down, then back at the group of women as if she just realized that she was still standing. She frowned, cleared her throat, and dropped into her chair.

"Now," Edna said, switching to a cheerful tone as she began to rifle through one of the baskets on the coffee table. "Who wants to get started on this *boppli* blanket?"

Chapter Thirteen

The next day, Emma tried to slip through the Stoneybrook farmyard without being seen. She didn't want to risk running into any of Benjamin's sisters. The work frolic had been humiliating enough—and that was in her own home. Now, she was on their property. What would they say to her here?

Belinda honked a greeting, flapped her wings and settled into a plastic baby pool that Benjamin had bought for her. Emma had remembered to bring a treat to stay on the goose's good side and she stopped long enough to drop a handful of oats onto the ground. Belinda paddled to the edge of the pool, stretched out her long neck, and gobbled up the oats. She hopped out of the pool, waddled over to Emma, and pushed her bill against Emma's palm.

Emma patted her head. The white feathers felt soft as flower petals. "At least someone here wants me around." She fed Belinda the rest of the oats. Belinda honked when the food was gone, then waddled back to the pool and climbed in with a splash. A breeze whipped across the farmyard and golden leaves flew past Emma as she walked the rest of the way to the barn. She was just about to pull open the battered wooden door when she heard Amanda's voice.

"I just don't think it's a *gut* idea."

Emma froze. She had a bad feeling inside that Amanda was talking about her. "You should have heard Viola yesterday." That voice belonged to Miriam. Emma sighed. Of course it did.

"Viola is always full of talk," Benjamin said. "It doesn't matter."

"Of course it does. This could affect your future."

Benjamin snorted. "That's *lecherich*."

"*Nee*, it's not ridiculous, Benji," Amanda said gently. "This could hurt your chances with other women in the future."

"Then let it."

Emma felt a bolt of joy shoot through her. Had Benjamin really said that? Did he care about her that much? Sure, he was just a friend—but what a wonderful friend.

There was a heavy sigh. "Benji, you can't mean that."

"Sure, I can."

Emma knew that she should either let them

know she was here or walk away, but she felt frozen, unable to move.

"Do you understand how much we love you?" Miriam asked.

Benjamin didn't respond.

"We love Emma too," Amanda added quickly.

"Funny way of showing it," Benjamin cut in.

"But she's not our responsibility," Amanda said. "You are. We just want you to be happy. Life is hard enough without making it harder through a difficult match. Can't you see that? Your life would be a lot harder with her. It doesn't have to be that way."

"You don't know that," Benjamin said.

"It's common sense, Benji," Miriam said. "A child that's not yours, a *fraa* who's a loose cannon that's already gone *Englisch* once—these are not the foundations for an easy life."

"There are so many other *gut* women in Bluebird Hills," Amanda said. "There just isn't any reason to choose one who would make your life harder."

"Look, even if what you're saying is true—which it's not—we're not together. We're just friends. So it doesn't matter."

"If it doesn't matter, then why not cut back on how much time you're spending together?" Miriam asked.

Emma's heart pounded in her ears as she waited for the answer.

Footsteps padded across the barn floor, followed by a loud bark. Paws scratched at the barn door. More barking.

"There's someone there," Benjamin said.

Emma swallowed hard. She should not have stood there for so long. Ollie whined at the door. Emma forced a pleasant expression on her face and eased the door open. The rusty hinges creaked as the dog pushed through and sniffed her hand. "It's just me, *bu*." His tail thumped against the doorjamb.

"Emma!" Miriam turned to stare from where she stood beside her brother and sister.

"You're here early," Amanda said. She and Miriam both looked embarrassed. They knew they had been caught.

"I'm sorry you had to hear that," Benjamin said.

"*Ach, nee.* I didn't hear…much."

Miriam stepped forward. Her expression quickly shifted to determination. "We were just saying it's probably best to slow things down here. You know, cut back on how much you're working."

Benjamin frowned. "*Nee.*"

"*Vell*, we were about to agree that—"

"*Nee.* You and Amanda agreed. I didn't and I

won't." He strode over to Emma and threw his arm around her shoulder. He had never seemed so strong or self-assured as he stared his sisters down with a steady, even gaze. Emma didn't know whether to grin or melt into his arms. She did know that her entire body had turned to jelly. She wasn't sure that her knees could support her. If it weren't for his strong, firm arm around her, she might have collapsed. It wasn't every day that the man you love stands up for you like this.

Love?

Yes. This was love. It could not be anything else. In fact, it probably never had been anything else. The realization shot through her like electricity.

"Emma is here to work with me today. And that is what we are going to do. And she's going to keep coming over for as long as she can. I can't do this without her. You both know that." He hesitated. "And you also know she's my best friend. She's *willkumme* here anytime, whether or not she's here to work." He looked down at Emma. His eyes were so close that she could see the black flecks within the deep brown irises. She had never noticed how full and thick his eyelashes were before. His chest rose and fell against her side. He was breathing fast. She knew how much this was costing him. He hated conflict. But he cared about her more than his need to avoid it.

Miriam gave a curt nod. "*Oll recht.* I understand. You're always *willkumme*, Emma. I didn't mean to make it seem otherwise."

Emma did not know what to say to that, so she said nothing.

"I've got a blackberry pie coming out of the oven in about twenty minutes," Amanda said. "You're both *willkumme* to *kumme* over to the house and have some when it's ready." But the strained tone to her voice didn't match the inviting words.

"No, thank you," Benjamin said as they filed past him. He waited to drop his arm until they shut the door behind them. Then he pulled away from Emma, as if he had just noticed what he had done. He cleared his throat.

"At least they're trying," Emma said, trying to steer attention away from the fact that his arm had just been around her—and how much she had liked it.

Benjamin sighed. "Are they?"

"I really appreciated that you stood up for me. *Danki.*"

His eyes bore into hers. "You don't have to thank me. It was the right thing to do. You deserve respect."

Emma wondered what he meant by that. Had

he defended her simply because he was a *gut*, honorable man, or because he had feelings for her that went beyond friendship? It certainly had felt like the latter when his arm was around her and his deep brown eyes were gazing into hers with so much intensity.

But now, she was not so sure. After all, she had overheard him tell his sisters that he and Emma were just friends.

Emma had never been so confused, or so sure of her own feelings.

No one spoke at the dinner table that evening. Miriam passed the blue porcelain bowl of mashed potatoes around the table and each sibling scooped out a serving without saying a word. Benjamin picked up his knife and fork and cut into his country-style steak. Outside, Ollie barked in the distance. A goat bleated from inside the barn and wind howled against the old farmhouse, sending the chimes on the front porch ringing.

"What's gotten into everybody?" Leah finally asked. She picked up her glass of lemonade, drank a long sip, and set it down again. "What did I miss?"

"The usual," Benjamin said.

Miriam set down her fork. "We should talk about it."

"Nothing left to say," Benjamin said. The room fell back into silence.

It was a very long dinner.

The next morning, Benjamin grabbed his ham biscuits while they were still on the tray, hot from the oven. He wrapped them in a dish towel and headed outside before Miriam could say anything to him. He didn't want to hear another word. Unless she was ready to treat Emma with respect. Otherwise, enough was enough.

He went through his chores automatically, without thinking. After scratching Lilli behind the ears and patting her neck, he led her onto the milking platform and attached the diesel milking machine. He repeated the process until Leah showed up. "Milking's almost done," he said. "Just those two to go." He nodded at a black goat and a spotted one who were waiting their turn.

"You're never early to milking. You should have waited for me instead of doing it all yourself."

Benjamin shrugged.

"Better to do all the milking yourself than eat breakfast with Miriam?"

Benjamin grunted. "Something like that."

Leah sat down on a milking stool and sighed. "Do you want to talk about it?"

"*Nee.*"

Leah laughed. "*Oll recht*, but are you *going* to talk about it?"

Benjamin shrugged again.

"Would you stop shrugging and grunting? The goats are communicating better than you this morning."

"Nothing to say, I guess."

"*Ach*, I think you have plenty to say."

"They don't want Emma around."

"I know. I've tried to talk to them about it."

"They usually listen to you. *Vell*, more than they listen to me, anyway."

Leah shook her head. "Not this time."

"Emma heard Miriam and Amanda talking about her."

"Oh no."

"Yep. I did what I could but…" He held up his hands. "I'll be surprised if she comes back today. She knows they don't want her here."

"You know, you could tell her how you feel."

Benjamin flinched. "You're changing the subject."

"No sense wasting time when it needs to be said."

"You sound like Eliza Zook."

Leah laughed. "Maybe I should try to be more assertive like her." She gave Benjamin a meaningful look. "Maybe we both should."

"I stood up for Emma yesterday. And I'll do it again."

"I know you will. But maybe it's time for more, now."

Benjamin scratched his jaw. "She doesn't feel that way about me."

"How can you be sure?"

"She's said so."

"Really? You sure about that?"

"*Ya*. I'm sure. Pretty sure."

"Just pretty sure?"

"Completely sure."

Leah raised an eyebrow.

"She's out of my league, Leah. We all know that."

"Don't sell yourself short, Benji. You don't know what women want if you think you don't have anything to offer."

"Women want men like Gabriel King who are *gut* at everything. Men who are charming and athletic, who can fix things, put in a hard day's work. You know, *that* kind of man."

"I remember back when Gabriel was a complete slacker."

"He was always athletic."

"That's really not the point."

"Leah, stop trying to make me feel better."

Leah leaned forward and rested her elbows on her knees. "Look, if Emma doesn't love you for who you are—including your disabilities—then she was never right for you and never could be."

"She doesn't love me."

"*Vell*, you'll never know with this attitude."

"I'm not having an attitude. I'm being realistic."

Leah made a sound in the back of her throat. "Stop selling her short. She's a woman of faith. She sees your worth, just like you see hers."

Benjamin didn't know what to say to that. He made a show of checking the milking machine.

"You know I'm right, Benji."

"*Oll recht.* I'll think about saying something."

What if Leah was right? He would never know unless he took the risk. Hope flickered within him, like a tiny flame finding oxygen. But the doubt was still there too. "She was certain sure quick to say we were just friends when we went to the Old Amish Kitchen the other night."

"Maybe she's afraid that you don't love her."

Benjamin laughed out loud and startled a goat. The animal jumped, then bleated. "Steady now, old girl," he murmured. Then, to Leah he said, "Don't be *lecherich*."

"It's not ridiculous that a soon-to-be single *mamm* would assume that you wouldn't want a relationship with her."

Benjamin frowned. "You can't mean…" He shook his head. "Emma's popular. Everyone wants to court Emma."

"Not anymore," Leah said gently.

"Yeah, but…" He shifted his weight. "That doesn't mean she'd want to be with me all of the sudden. Or are you saying she'd settle for me because I'm her last shot?"

"*Nee!* I'm not saying that at all. I'm just trying to explain that she must be feeling rejected and ashamed. She's not going to feel lovable right now, Benji. So maybe she agreed that you're just friends because that was the way she thought you wanted it."

"Oh." Benjamin tried to ignore the way his heart was pounding against his throat. Could Emma possibly feel the same way about him as he felt about her? They had been drawing close, but…

"Just think about it, Benji."

"*Oll recht.* I will."

Leah stood up and stretched. "I'm going to go start on the laundry since you've got the milking handled." She began to walk away.

"Hey, Leah."

"*Ya?*"

"*Danki.*"

"Thank me by following my advice."

Benjamin kept thinking about what Leah said. There was no other conversation to distract him. The silence between him and his other sisters just kept growing. He and Amanda didn't talk as they led the goats to the south pasture to graze. He kept his mouth shut when he had to hold one of the Angoras still while Amanda checked her for a broken leg. Thankfully, it was just a sprain and they bandaged her up and sent her on her way. This was when they would normally exchange a satisfied look and feel good about a job well done. But instead, Benjamin felt the distance between them as the goat hobbled away to snack on a dandelion. There was no easy camaraderie, no small, shared victory.

Amanda started to head out of the pasture without him, but turned back. "Miriam's hurt, Benji."

He couldn't believe what he was hearing. "*She's* hurt? What about me?"

Amanda sighed. Her eyes looked sad. "You'll understand when you're older. At least I hope you will."

Benjamin shook his head. "I understand plenty now, Amanda."

She just sighed, turned away, and picked her way down the long, sloping hill. Her movements were quick and agile, as always. Benjamin watched and wished he could be as confident-looking as she was. Lilly bumped his leg and he reached down to pat her back. "They don't know what they're talking about." Lilly bleated and nudged his leg again. He crouched down to scratch behind her ears. When he stood back up again and scanned the pastureland, Amanda was no longer in sight. But he could feel the empty space she had left. The silence between him and his sisters hurt like a toothache, deep inside. He had no idea how to make them see what he did. And he had no idea how to stop the guilt, even though he had done nothing wrong. It wasn't his fault that Miriam was hurting. He had never asked her to take over as mother to all of them. And he certainly had never asked her to interfere in his relationship with Emma.

Even so, Miriam had sacrificed her youth for the family—for him. Now, she would probably never have a chance to marry, never have a family of her own. She had chosen him instead.

The thought sat heavily inside, as if he had drunk curdled milk. He could not ignore or push it away as much as he tried. And, all the while, he was still wondering how Emma really felt about him, and if she would show up for work that day.

Emma knew she was asking for trouble when she pinned a work kerchief over her bun and marched over to Stoneybrook Farm. She was carrying the baby low in her belly and she felt like Belinda, waddling across the farmyard. As soon as Emma saw Benjamin, she started to feel a little better. He flashed his signature grin and waved her over. But behind that smile, she caught the tension in his eyes.

Throughout the next hour, he kept pausing, as if he were about to say something, then he would clamp his mouth shut and frown. Emma wondered what he wanted to say to her. The quiet dread inside her began to grow. Was she forcing Benjamin to choose between her and his sisters? They weren't courting, but they *were* best friends. Clearly, even that was a line that Miriam did not want them to cross. Was Benjamin trying to get up the courage to ask Emma to leave? No, that didn't make sense. He had been so bold about standing up for her the day before.

A shout from the farmyard made Emma lose her train of thought.

Benjamin shot out of his folding chair.

Something was wrong. Emma slammed the accounting book shut and began hauling herself out of the chair. With a beach-ball-sized belly, it wasn't fast going. Benjamin stopped to help her up from her chair.

There was another shout.

"Go on," she said. "I'll catch up."

He nodded and jogged out of the barn.

Emma followed as fast as she could. When she rounded the corner of the barn, Lilli the goat was running past the clothesline set up in the middle of the farmyard, a clean white sheet caught over her back like a cape and a white pillowcase clasped in her mouth.

"Stop!" Benjamin shouted as he raced after her.

"My laundry!" Amanda shrieked.

Leah lunged for the goat, missed, and landed on the ground, flat on her stomach. Mud splattered her blue cape dress and leaves stuck to her *kapp*. "Now, I've got to do even more washing!" she wailed.

Miriam hitched up her skirt and began chasing Lilli in circles. She set her mouth in a thin line, creased her brow in concentration, and pumped her arms as her bare feet flew through the mud.

Emma's first instinct was to help and she started to take off into the muddy yard, but immediately remembered the extra bulk she was carrying and skidded to a stop. Sometimes she forgot that she was expecting. Her belly had gotten so big so quickly that it was easy to remember herself as she had been before, instead of as she was now.

Benjamin darted past the commotion and disappeared into the farmhouse. The screen door banged shut behind him as his sisters shouted after him.

"Benjamin! Get back here!"

"Where is he going?" Naomi shouted as she lunged at the goat and missed.

A few beats later, Benjamin flew back onto the porch, carrying a muffin. His straw hat flew off as he hurtled down the porch steps and sprinted to the clothesline. Lilli evaded Miriam, darted past Leah, and trotted over to Benjamin. "How about a blueberry muffin?" he asked as the goat stopped in front of him. She dropped the pillowcase in her mouth and gobbled the muffin down in two big bites. Benjamin reached down and grabbed hold of her as she chewed.

"Benji, what are you doing?" Miriam asked. She marched over and pulled the mud-stained sheet from Lilli's back, then stooped down to collect the pillowcase from the ground.

"Giving Lilli her favorite food."

"But I baked those for tomorrow's breakfast."

"*Vell*, did you want your laundry back or not? It's not my fault that blueberry muffins are Lilli's favorite food." He looked over at Emma and winked.

"How do you even know that's her favorite food, Benji?" Miriam studied the stained pillowcase. "Never mind. I don't want to know." She turned on her heels and strode toward the farmhouse.

"You're *willkumm*, Miriam!" Benjamin shouted after her.

She didn't answer.

"*Danki*, Benjamin," Leah said. "I should have thought of that."

Amanda and Naomi didn't say anything. They glanced at Emma, then at Benjamin. Emma could feel the tension in the air.

"I've got to get those muddy linens soaking before the stains set," Leah said. "Stay for dinner if you can, Emma." With a quick wave, she jogged to the farmhouse, up the porch steps, and disappeared inside with a bang of the screen door.

Amanda and Naomi followed her without ever acknowledging Benjamin. Emma knew that Benjamin didn't always get along with his sisters, but this felt different. No one had laughed or joked, even though the incident had been hilarious. They didn't even point out that Benjamin must have left the gate open again. Something hung in the air, unresolved between them. And it didn't take a genius to know what that was.

"They're upset with you because of me, ain't so?" Emma asked as soon as Benjamin's sisters were all out of earshot.

"*Ach, vell*, I don't know about that."

"Benjamin." Emma gave him a no-nonsense look.

"Leah invited you to stay for dinner."

"I'm not talking about Leah."

Benjamin sighed. "It's been a little tense since yesterday."

"After you stood up for me."

"Ya." He doubled back to where his straw hat lay on the ground, picked it up, and brushed the dirt off the brim. "But don't worry about that. It's fine. They'll come around. Eventually."

But they still had not come around by the next day, when Emma returned to Stoneybrook Farm. She had not stayed for dinner the night before, of course.

Benjamin was quiet and withdrawn as they worked together. She could see the situation was nibbling away at him. But when she asked if he was okay, he just smiled and said he was. When Miriam and Amanda ran into them in the production building, no one spoke. Benjamin's brow creased as he poured ingredients into the slow cooker and pretended that they weren't there. His sisters didn't chat or laugh with one another. Instead, they unloaded a cart of milk and adjusted dials on the machinery while Emma hunched over the counter, wishing that she were invisible. She had never felt such tension in the family before.

Miriam's and Amanda's black athletic shoes thudded against the concrete floor, breaking into the heavy silence as they filed outside. As soon as the heavy double doors thumped shut behind them, Emma let out a breath and turned to Benjamin. "When was the last time you spoke to them?"

He shrugged and shook a few drops of lavender oil into the slow cooker. "*Ach*, I don't know. That conversation in the barn, I guess."

"You haven't spoken since then?"

"Um, I did ask Naomi to pass the salt at dinner last night."

"That hardly counts." Emma wanted to say more. She wanted to encourage him to say something to Miriam. But that would open a big can of worms. Because Emma knew she, herself, was the problem. What advice could she give Benjamin, when she was the reason that he had fallen out with his sisters? She felt a chill and hugged herself, even though the day was warm and the sun was shining.

"Don't worry about it," Benjamin said. "It'll be *oll recht*."

"It doesn't seem like it."

Benjamin's jaw tightened. He hesitated.

"What is it?"

"It's nothing. I just… *Vell*, Miriam gave up a lot to take care of me when I was younger. I can't help but feel guilty."

"Have you ever talked to her about how you feel?"

"*Nee*, we don't talk about things like that."

"Maybe you should."

"I wouldn't know how." He fiddled with the temperature knob on the slow cooker. "And I don't know how she would react. I don't want to hurt her. I know she's tough to deal with some-times—and she's been out of line about you, certain sure—but this family is all she has and will probably be all that she ever has. It makes her…" He searched for the right word.

"Overprotective?"

"*Ya.* She worries. I don't think she ever got over our parents' deaths. It's like she's afraid that if she doesn't hold on to all of us tightly enough, she'll lose us too."

Emma swiveled on her stool to look into Benjamin's eyes. How had she never noticed the depth that they held before? "That's an astute observation. I don't think many people in your situation would have that level of empathy."

Benjamin just shrugged and picked up a vial of basil essential oil. "What do you think about lavender basil?" He unscrewed the lid and sniffed. "Would that make a *gut* combination?"

Emma knew that Benjamin was changing the subject, but she could not shake what he had said. She was coming between him and his only family. And the guilt of that division was eating him up inside. He had chosen her, but now he was paying the price.

Emma continued to think about it after she got home that evening. She recalled Benjamin's conflicted expression while she washed the dishes and put them away. She remembered the sadness in his eyes as she unpinned her bun and let her hair down. And, after she blew out the kerosene lamp and lay beneath the quilt in the darkness, Emma thought about how quiet he had become around her. It was as if he wanted to say something to her and couldn't. Did he regret standing up for her?

Emma turned over beneath the quilt. An owl hooted outside the window and wind whispered through the orchard. The baby moved inside her and Emma fell asleep holding her belly as she tried to figure out how to make things better for Benjamin.

When the sun rose, she had a splitting headache that kept her home from the church service. The stress was making her sick. Spending the day in bed gave her plenty of time to think. When Monday morning rolled around and she was due back at Stoneybrook Farm, Emma had decided there was only one solution. Without her, Benjamin could go back to his happy, carefree life. He would mend the conflict with his sisters and everything would be all right.

Well, not for her. But that was okay. She cared more about making things better for Benjamin.

He would have been better off if she had never come back to town. Miriam's words echoed inside her mind, *"Life is hard enough without making it harder through a difficult match."* Emma buried her face in the pillow and squeezed her eyes closed, trying to shut out the memory. *"A child that's not yours."*

She wasn't just coming between Benjamin and his sisters. She had been longing for a life together that would not be good for him. What if he had fallen in love with her, as she had with him? Would that really be best for him? Should she expect him to raise another man's child? Should she allow him to damage his reputation by marrying a fallen woman? No. She should not. She loved Benjamin and love meant doing what was best for the other person.

Emma kicked off the quilt and sat up. She knew exactly what she had to do. She just wished that it wasn't going to break her heart.

Chapter Fourteen

◥◣◢◤

Emma didn't show up at Stoneybrook Farm that day. Benjamin waited in the production building for an hour before he clicked off the slow cooker and wandered outside. The bright sunlight hurt his eyes and he shielded his brow with the blade of his hand as he scanned the stretch of land that led to the Yoder property. He realized that he had forgotten his hat and doubled back into the production building, swiped it off the counter, and marched back outside. Now, the sun didn't feel as harsh and he could see clearly when he stared down the hill. Ollie trotted over, circled once, then headed toward the fence that separated the farms.

"*Ya.* I was just thinking the same thing." Benjamin walked to the gate, remembered to shut it behind him, and headed down the hill. Ollie barked at being left behind before catching a scent and trotting away, nose to the ground, tail whipping from side to side. Benjamin hoped that Emma had been delayed because she had something else to do. Maybe she was caught up with the laundry, or had a pie in the oven that she couldn't leave. But he knew that didn't make sense. She was avoiding him.

Then a new thought shot through him, as sharp and cold as a knife. What if she was in trouble? What if the baby was coming? He picked up his pace, stumbling down the hill until he reached the vegetable garden. He skidded to a stop as another idea struck him. If the baby were coming then he shouldn't be here. But what if she needed help? What if something else was wrong?

Or what if she was just avoiding him?

Benjamin set his mouth in a grim line and marched around to the front of the farmhouse. There was only one way to find out.

He was surprised how quickly the door swung open after he knocked, as if Emma had been waiting for him. He glanced down at her belly, then felt foolish. It's not like he would be able to tell if she were in labor. "Are you… Are you *oll recht*?" His eyes moved down to her belly again.

"Oh." Emma's hand moved to her baby bump when she noticed where he was looking. "That. *Ya*, I'm fine. Everything's *oll recht*."

Benjamin felt a wave of relief. *"Gut."* He blotted his forehead with his shirtsleeve. The shaded porch felt unusually hot for autumn. "I was worried when you didn't show up today."

Emma swallowed and looked away.

Oh no. He could see the guilt and conflict in her eyes. As if the world were unfolding in slow motion, he knew what she was about to say, but was powerless to stop it. He could just stand there, trapped in the moment, wishing that he could stop it from happening.

"I can't help you with the soap-making business anymore, Benji." She was still looking away. "I'm sorry."

The words hit him like a punch. He had been living for those afternoons spent together. It was the first thing he thought about when he woke up in the morning. He looked forward to it all day, as he did his chores. It was the last thing he thought about at night as he drifted off to sleep, remembering how they had laughed together, hoping that he had made her happy. "Right," he managed to stammer. "*Oll recht.* Of course. You've got a lot to deal with and the *boppli* will be here soon."

Emma swallowed hard. "*Ya.* The *boppli.* I have to take it easy now."

Benjamin knew that might be true. But there was more going on than that. Otherwise, she would have come over to tell him. And she would be able to meet his eyes right now. Emma was hiding the real reason. Was it that his sisters had pushed her away? No, Emma had been dealing with that ever since she started working with him. Why would she avoid them now, when he had just stood up for her?

That's what hurt the most. He had stood up for her, had chosen her over his sisters, and it had not been enough. Because he was not enough. He would do it again, of course, simply because it had been the right thing to do. But it still hurt. It hurt so badly that he could actually feel the emotion as a physical pain, burning beneath his breastbone.

"I understand," he said. Because he did. She could not love him, not the way he loved her. It was time to let go of that dream, let her go on and live her life. He needed to give her the space to find a father for her baby.

But he had not expected it to all come crashing down today. He was not prepared. It took a moment for him to get any more words out. "I guess I better get going," he finally managed after an awkward silence. "There's wood that needs chopping. See you around, *ya*?" But he knew that he would not.

Benjamin did not go straight home after that. He walked over to the sunflower field and wandered through the tall stalks, alone. Bees buzzed nearby and the dirt felt soft beneath his feet. A flock of Canada geese flew overhead in a V, their dark silhouettes contrasted against the brilliant blue sky. He wanted Emma to be there with him, like she used to be. He wanted to ask her where she thought the geese were going and daydream about going there together. He wanted to ask her about her day and hear her thoughts on the shade of red that the Glicks had just painted their barn. Some folks thought it was too fancy.

Instead, he drifted over to the lake and sank down onto the bank. The ground felt damp, but he didn't mind. He looked out over the water and wondered how everything with Emma had fallen apart so quickly. Had he been too pushy to ask her to go to the Old Amish Kitchen with him? Had she gotten the idea that he wanted to be more than friends and was trying to let him down gently? Or had she just been too tired to deal with his sisters anymore? He would stand up for her again. He could go back and tell her that he would make them accept her.

No. Because then he would have to admit how much he loved her.

Benjamin sighed, plucked a dandelion, and tore the stem into small pieces. The lake reflected the orange and yellow leaves on the trees that towered overhead. A few leaves floated on the surface, like small, lazy boats. He watched as a yellow one pirouetted through the air to land gently on the water.

Benjamin threw down what was left of the

dandelion and brushed his hands off on his trousers. He wanted to propose to Emma. He wanted to march down to her house, bang on the door, and tell her how much he loved her—how much he had always loved her.

But that wouldn't be fair to her. He was her friend. She trusted him. If he told her how he felt, she might feel pressured. She was alone, about to be an unwed mother. He wanted to be there for her and the baby, but only if she wanted him to be. He didn't want her to feel that she had to accept a proposal because it was her only option. If she wanted to marry him, he would know. It would have been obvious.

No, she wanted to be left alone. She had just told him that, hadn't she? He would respect her wishes. That was what you did when you loved a woman. You respected her.

He just wished it didn't hurt so much to let her go.

He dreaded going home because he would have to face his sisters. They would know that they had been right. But the chores had to get done, whether or not he wanted to do them. So, as the sunset painted the lake pink and gold, he sighed, stood up, and walked back home with slouched shoulders and an aching chest.

Benjamin could not avoid Amanda in the milking shed. Then, to make everything worse,

Miriam and Naomi strolled in. They all worked side by side, ignoring one another.

Leah poked her head inside the doorway as she wiped her hands on a rag. "Hey, Benji, is Emma *oll recht*?"

Miriam frowned. "Did something happen?"

"She didn't *kumme* over today," Leah said. "She's not in labor, is she?"

"*Nee*. She just can't work here anymore."

Naomi tucked a loose strand of dark hair beneath her work kerchief. "Did she say why?"

Benjamin shrugged and tried to keep his focus on the goat on the milking platform. He didn't want to see the smug look on his sisters' faces. But when he snuck a peek at Miriam, she didn't look smug at all. She started to say something, then closed her mouth and went back to frowning. The diesel-powered milking machines hummed softly in the background. One of the goats stomped her little hoof. Benjamin wished someone would say something. The silence was worse than arguing.

"I'm sorry, Benjamin," Leah said. "We should have made her feel more *willkumme*."

"*You* did make her feel *willkumme*," Benjamin said, then gave Miriam a pointed look.

Miriam exhaled. "I've got to get the turkey potpie out of the oven. Can you take over here, Leah?"

"Ya."

When they sat down to eat, the pie should have been delicious, but Benjamin had lost his appetite. Everything tasted like sawdust. Everything *felt* like sawdust without Emma. He had been okay before she had come back to town. But then he let himself fall into a dream. Spending every day with her had ruined him. Now, he could not imagine being without her.

But he would manage it, because he would respect her wishes. Simple as that.

The next morning, Benjamin noticed Miriam watching him as he pushed his eggs and bacon around on his plate. She said nothing when he left the table early to start on his chores. By lunch, his stomach was rumbling and he managed to eat half a slice of leftover turkey potpie, but it didn't taste as good as it should have. He pushed away from the table and dropped his napkin beside his plate.

"You have to eat, Benji," Miriam said.

"I'm fine."

"You're not fine."

"Vell, you've gotten your way, so you're happy at least." He stood up, pushed in his chair, carried his plate to the counter, and dropped it in the big farmhouse sink before marching to the door. He waited for Miriam to snap back at him,

but she stayed silent. He could feel her watching him the entire time.

Benjamin was in the south pasture that afternoon when he saw Miriam striding up the long, gentle incline that led to the high point of their property. Green fields and pastures spread out around her, dotted with an occasional tree covered in golden leaves. The creek caught the sunlight as water splashed over the rocks. The goats bleated and the bells around their necks rang as they grazed. Benjamin took off his straw hat, wiped the sweat from his brow, and replaced it as he watched Miriam approach. It was a long walk, so there was plenty of time for him to dread whatever conversation they were about to have.

"They've almost eaten all the grass in this pasture," Miriam said when she finally reached him.

So, she was going to start with small talk. Interesting. That meant she was nervous. Otherwise, she wouldn't bother.

"We'll have to move them over to the west field, soon."

"*Ya.*" Benjamin scratched his elbow. "You don't usually *kumme* up here."

"*Nee*, because I know you're taking care of everything up this way."

Benjamin narrowed his eyes. That almost

sounded like a compliment. And that made him suspicious. "So why are you here?"

"I looked for you in the production building, but you're not making soap today."

"Nee."

"You're not going to quit, are you?" She had to tilt her head up to meet his eyes.

He shrugged. "It doesn't matter anymore."

"Of course it does."

He shrugged again.

"You're not eating. You're not working—"

"I'm getting all the farm work done."

"That's not what I meant." She shook her head. "I didn't *kumme* here to fight."

Benjamin raised his eyebrows.

Miriam pinched the bridge of her nose and squeezed her eyes shut. "I know that's what you're expecting." She lowered her hand, opened her eyes, and looked up at him. "I can see how much you're hurting. I've been... I haven't..."

"Ya?" Benjamin's lips curled up on one side in a slight smile. Miriam sounded like she was about to apologize. "Go on."

"Ach, fine." She glared at him. "I've been too hard on you."

"And?"

"And on Emma."

Benjamin's half smile became a grin. "Now

this is unexpected. Miriam Stoltzfus admitting she's wrong."

"Don't push it, Benjamin."

"You only call me Benjamin when you're scared. Remember when I was little and you'd shout out 'Benjamin' if I got too close to the lake because you thought I'd drown."

"*Ya.* Of course I remember. And I'm still scared that you'll drown."

"I know. That's why I used that example. Maybe I'm smarter than you think."

"I know how smart you are."

"Not smart enough to choose the right *fraa* though, ain't so?"

Miriam exhaled. "Can we sit down? I can't stand here craning my neck to look up at you."

Benjamin chuckled. "Little Miriam."

"Ha. Ha. Very funny." She smoothed the back of her dress and sank down onto the grassy hillside. Benjamin sat down beside her, folded his legs, and rested his elbows on his knees. They stared out over the rolling hills and the sunflower field, far away. The yellow flowers were a soft blur, all blended together in the distance. "You can see all the way down to the lake from here," Miriam said.

"*Ya.* I know." He looked over at her. "You didn't know that?"

"I guess I forgot. Life gets so busy, I forget to

pay attention to what's important." She motioned toward the sparkling blue water at the bottom of the long, sloped stretch of farmland. "So, as I was saying, I was always afraid you'd drown in that. You and Emma just wouldn't stay away."

Benjamin smiled at the memory. *"Ya."*

Miriam elbowed him. "You're smiling, but I certain sure wasn't. I was afraid."

"Just because you lost Mamm and Daed doesn't mean you're going to lose me."

Miriam stiffened. "How did you know…"

"I thought we just agreed that I'm smart, remember?"

Miriam laughed. "Right." The smile faded quickly. "I didn't realize you know how much I worry."

"I've lived with you all these years, haven't I?"

"Is it that obvious?"

"Ya."

Miriam ran her fingers over her apron, smoothing invisible wrinkles. "It was such a shock. No one expects to lose Amish parents in a car accident. I trusted their hired driver. I wasn't prepared."

"No one could have been."

"I felt like I should have been. I wanted to be stronger for you."

"You were."

"I hope I still am." She turned to face him.

"That's why I can't let you drown now. You made it through childhood, but the world is even more dangerous now. Decisions that you make now will determine the rest of your life."

"I'm not going to drown."

"Love can drown anyone."

"Only if you're in love with the wrong person."

Miriam hesitated. "You're in love with her." She said it as a statement, not a question, and studied Benjamin's reaction.

He met her gaze. "*Ya.* I am."

She nodded. "I thought it was a crush for a long time. But I can see otherwise, now."

They both looked away from one another. "I wanted you to be happy," Miriam said quietly. "And I tried so hard to make sure you'd be happy that I ruined your chance at happiness. I'm sorry."

"What are you trying to say?"

"I drove Emma away. I should have accepted her. I'm sorry," she repeated.

Benjamin took a moment to process the apology. "*Danki* for saying that. It means a lot."

"I saw how happy you two made each other. And I see how it's affected you now that she's gone. I shouldn't have let it come to this." Miriam swallowed hard. "I just kept thinking that I can't lose you. That I can't let you drown."

Benjamin put his hand on her arm, squeezed, and let go. "I know, Miriam. I get it." One of the goats wandered past and the bell around her neck clanged as she lowered her head to graze. "And I hope *you* get it—really get it—that she's a *gut* woman. That she's *gut* for *me*."

Miriam sighed. "*Ya.* I get it. I was wrong to think that she would hurt you. Or that you couldn't handle being a *daed*. The truth is, that wasn't what I was most afraid of, deep down." She stopped talking and picked at a loose thread on her sleeve.

"Go on."

"It's like I said. I've been afraid of losing you. You're grown now. I have to let you go. And then what? I don't know what to do with my life if my purpose isn't to take care of you and your sisters anymore."

"Oh."

"Didn't see that one coming?"

"Not exactly."

"I guess I'll just have to figure it out."

"You will. You figured out how to get us this far, ain't so?"

Miriam smiled, but her eyes were far away. "*Ya.* I did."

Benjamin picked a blade of grass from the hillside and nibbled the end of it.

"Guess I better get back to my chores," Miriam said, but she made no move to get up.

Benjamin pulled the blade of grass out of his mouth and glanced over at her.

"You know you didn't ruin anything. Not really. Emma isn't in love with me. Nothing you did or didn't do was going to change that."

Miriam looked at him with a strange expression. "You really believe that, don't you?"

"Of course I do." He threw down the blade of grass. "Because it's true."

"I wouldn't be so sure about that," Miriam said.

"Why not?"

"I've seen the way she looks at you."

Chapter Fifteen

The days passed slowly. Emma missed Benjamin so much that it became an unrelenting ache in her chest. Amos and Edna watched her with concerned eyes. They whispered in corners when they thought she couldn't hear, then clamped their mouths shut and tried to smile when she caught them. Emma made an effort to keep a daily routine. She collected vegetables from the garden, swept and dusted, spent time in the orchards with Amos. He was considerate enough to pretend that she was a big help, even though Emma knew that she was too distracted and too tired to be much use to anyone. But she liked wandering the orchards with her uncle. The fruit hung heavy and nearly ripe, like little round treasures waiting to be plucked. She liked it best when the sunlight streamed through the branches in the late afternoon, casting a bright, golden glow around each pear. Sometimes it seemed like a fairy tale, everything glittering with sunlight, the bees humming softly in the background, the earth soft and damp beneath her bare feet.

And then she would remember. There would be no fairy-tale ending for her. Women in her situation did not get happily-ever-afters. They had to live with the shame and loneliness. She started watching the fence line that separated her from Stoneybrook Farm, hoping to see Benjamin's silhouette on the hill. But she never saw him.

More days passed, until the never-ending ache turned into a sharper pain on Sunday morning. Emma did not think it was anything to pay attention to. It was just something else to push down and ignore, like her need to be loved and valued by a good Amish husband.

Amos and Edna had to leave early because the service was in a farmhouse on the far side of the church district. The buggy ride would be longer than usual. "I can stay here," Edna said when Emma explained that she wasn't feeling well enough to go. "It might be close to your time."

"*Nee.* At my appointment on Friday, the midwife said there aren't any signs yet, remember?"

Edna nodded, but she did not look convinced.

"First babies don't come quickly," Emma said. "I wish they did. That's a problem I wouldn't mind having. Imagine coming home from church and I've got a *boppli* waiting for you."

Edna laughed. "You're right, I'm being silly.

It's hard not to worry. Are you sure you're *oll recht* for me to leave you alone?"

"Nothing is going to happen in the next few hours. You'll be home by this afternoon."

Edna studied Emma for a moment, then gave a decisive nod. "You're right. But promise me that you won't do anything but rest."

"Of course. It's Sunday."

Edna smiled. "But even on Sunday, there are farm chores that have to be done. Stay off your feet. Wait for us to *kumme* home and do them."

"*Oll recht.* I will."

"Promise?"

"Promise."

Edna hesitated, then switched to a crisp, clean Sunday apron before slipping out the front door. Amos trailed behind her. He took his best-for-Sunday black felt hat from the peg on the wall, dropped it onto his bald head, and pushed his last few strands of hair into place beneath the brim. "We'll be home soon," he said. "Take it easy while you can."

Emma pondered his advice as she listened to the steady clip-clop of hooves moving away and fading into silence. Everything would change soon. She was ready to meet her baby, but she wasn't ready to do it all alone. Of course, she would have Amos's and Edna's support. That meant the world to her. But it wasn't the same as having a life partner to share the joy and sorrow, to grow with, laugh with, a best friend who truly understood her. Well, that was asking too much. Some things simply weren't meant to be.

She settled onto the wicker rocker in the living room and picked up her knitting basket. She wanted to finish the baby booties before it was too late. They would look so cute on her baby's little feet. Emma felt better as she imagined those tiny feet and hands, the way her baby would snuggle against her and love her like no one else. She could hardly wait. But, at the same time, she wanted to keep the baby safe and sound, inside her. She was overwhelmed at the thought of it all being real.

As Emma knitted, she watched the leaves rustling in the orchard outside. A dog barked in the distance. She wondered if it were Ollie. A bird flew past the window and sailed away, into the sun.

By midmorning, Emma had not eaten. She felt too hot and stuffy, too nauseous. And the pain in her abdomen was growing. It had spread to her back. She told herself to stop thinking about it. She managed to convince herself it wasn't labor, until the pain began to sharpen into peaks, with spaces in between.

She was having contractions.

Emma stood up and clenched her hands into

fists, until her fingernails dug into her palms. This hurt worse than it should. Something was wrong. No, she reminded herself. Babies hurt. This was what Edna and Viola had warned her about. They had told her that it would hurt more than she could imagine.

Well, she would just have to wait for Edna to come back. She glanced at the wall clock. Only a few more hours, hopefully. If they didn't get caught up with a problem that needed solving. Amos could never say no to someone in need. Maybe she should call the midwife. But that would be a long walk to the phone shanty. Normally, they took the buggy for that. She would just have to wait it out here.

A pain gripped her so hard that it took her breath. Her midsection was being crushed by an invisible iron hand. Emma staggered forward and her water broke. It took her a moment to register what was happening. She needed help. The baby was coming. She could not wait.

Emma did not think to put on her shoes. Her brain felt slow and strange, as if she were watching what was happening, rather than experiencing it. She forgot to close the door behind her. Her bare feet padded down the porch steps, the old wooden boards creaking beneath her weight. She would go to Stoneybrook Farm. There was a shortcut through the property to the phone shanty. She wouldn't try to walk the long way, along the highway. If the Stoltzfuses were home, she could use the phone in the production building, the one they only used for business. But they would all be at the church service and the building would be locked up tight.

Grass whispered under her bare feet as she cut across the yard. When another pain stabbed through her abdomen, she stopped, braced her hands against her knees, and waited it out. She gritted her teeth. She would not cry. She would not think about how alone she was. There were a few *Englisch* neighbors, but they lived several miles down the highway. And they would probably be at their own church services, anyway. "*Gott,* help me to do this," Emma prayed as soon as the pain eased up enough for her to speak.

The irony of it flashed through her mind. Of course she was alone. This was the start of being a single mother, of being alone for what might be a lifetime. She would have to be strong.

The hill was steeper than it had been the last time she climbed it. Her breath came hard and fast. Her knees were weak and wobbly. Whenever the pain hit, she had to stop, freeze, and dig her fingernails into her palms. She didn't count how close the contractions were. She was afraid to know.

Ollie greeted her at the gate. She leaned on it

for a moment to catch her breath. Sweat dripped down her forehead and she wiped it from her eyes. Ollie whined as his tail darted back and forth slowly, low to the ground. He could sense something was wrong.

"I wish you could go to the phone shanty for me," Emma said.

Ollie whined louder.

Emma passed through the gate, leaned her back against it, and sank slowly down, until she reached the soft, damp ground. *I'll just rest for a minute*, she thought. *Just a minute. To catch my breath.*

Ollie barked. He sniffed her hands, trotted away, then paced back to her and barked again. "I wish Benjamin were home," she said. "But it's just you and me, Ollie."

Ollie barked and nudged Emma's shoulder.

"I can't get up just yet. Give me another minute."

Belinda honked and waddled across the farmyard. She honked again and looked at Emma quizzically. A goat wandered closer and Belinda hissed. The goat bleated and backed away. Belinda waddled closer to Emma and circled her protectively. Between crescendos of pain, Emma sensed that Ollie and Belinda were looking out for her. But the realization felt dim and far away.

She had to get to the phone.

* * *

Benjamin fiddled with the ace bandage on his ankle. The sprain wasn't too bad, but it was enough to keep him home from the church service. He had tripped over a pail in the milking shed and had not been able to catch his balance in time. He was embarrassed to admit what had happened—yet another clumsy accident. Having to explain it to everyone was keeping him from church more than the pain. It was only a dull throb now. He would be back on his feet soon, as long as he gave his ankle a rest today.

He was slumped on the couch with his foot propped on a crate stamped with the words *Yoder Orchards* when he heard the commotion. Ollie was barking. Belinda was honking. A goat was bleating. Benjamin frowned and pushed himself up. He hoped the fox wasn't back. He eased his foot to the ground, winced, and grabbed the old crutch propped against the couch. He had pulled it from the back of the closet after his little accident this morning. A spare crutch was always a handy thing to keep around.

He hobbled across the living room and managed to pull open the front door without losing his balance or letting his bad foot touch the floor. The screen door creaked and a blast of cool, crisp air met him. "Ollie," he shouted. "What's the matter?"

He saw Emma huddled against the fence and panic shot through him. "Emma!" He stumbled down the porch steps and tore across the farmyard. Somewhere along the way, he lost his crutch, but kept going. The pain in his ankle felt dim and far away, numbed by adrenaline. He dropped to the ground beside Emma as soon as he reached her. "I'm here. It's going to be *oll recht*."

Emma raised her head to look at him. Her face was unnaturally pale, her lips tight. Sweat beaded on her forehead even though the air was chilly. "The baby's coming," she whispered. "Fast." She closed her eyes, breathed in and out, as if it took all her concentration to speak. "Too fast."

"It's all right. I've got you now." He braced his hands beneath her and hefted her up, until she was cradled in his arms. "You're safe now." She murmured something he couldn't understand as she turned her face into his chest. Pain shot up Benjamin's leg. He clenched his jaw and forced himself to ignore it. Emma and her baby were all that mattered now. He could feel her heartbeat against his body and the soft, warm sigh of her breath against his neck. Then her muscles tightened and she inhaled in a jagged gasp. He held her closer. "I'm going to call the midwife. This will be over soon." He wished he could take the pain away from her. He wished he could be the one to hurt instead of her. If he could trade her for it, he would.

He limped across the farmyard, each step sending a bolt of agony up his leg. But he knew his pain was nothing compared with what Emma was suffering. He paused at the porch steps, gathered his strength, and forced his way up, leaning and sliding against the railing to help offset some of the weight from his ankle.

Emma stirred in his arms and he tightened his grip around her. "We're almost inside," he said as he adjusted her weight enough to free one hand to pull open the screen door. It banged shut behind him as his footsteps thudded hard and fast across the worn floorboards.

"I didn't think you'd be here," Emma murmured.

"I'll always be here for you," Benjamin said. He laid her gently onto the couch, then lifted her head and placed a cushion beneath it. He didn't want to let her go. He wanted to keep holding her forever. But he eased away. "I'm going to call the midwife. I'll be nearby and I'll be back soon."

"Hurry," she said.

That word reverberated inside Benjamin's head as he limped back outside. The pain in his ankle was sharper and brighter now. He tried to keep his weight off it as he hobbled down the steps, gripping the railing beneath white knuckles. *Hurry.* He managed to grab his crutch from the farmyard as he rushed toward the production building. He had never been so thankful that Miriam had installed a telephone. Amos and the elders had approved it, since it was for business only.

And now, for emergencies.

Benjamin's crutch banged loudly against the concrete floor as he hurried across the large, echoing space to the office area. Benjamin knew the midwife's name—all the women in the church district called on her to deliver their babies—but he didn't know her number. He pulled the thick phone book from the metal drawer and began flipping through it. He could hear his breath hissing in and out and feel his heartbeat pulsing. *Hurry.* He said the ABCs in his head, then flipped back from the *V* pages to the *T* pages. He saw the word *Troyer* at the top of the page, stabbed it with his finger, and traced downward. There it was. Troyer, Elizabeth. He jerked the phone from the cradle and punched in the numbers. His fingers drummed against the desk as the phone rang. Once, twice, three times. "*Please, Gott,*" he whispered.

"Hello, this—"

"*Kumme* quick. Emma Yoder is in labor. She's

alone. I mean, it's just me here. We're at Stoney-brook Farm next door to the Yoders."

"Benjamin? Is this you?"

"*Ya*, it's Benjamin. Hurry."

"I'm on my way."

Benjamin did not take the time to say good-bye. He slammed the phone into the cradle and limped back across the production building. The tap, tap, tap of his crutch echoed against the high ceiling. *Hurry.* He pushed himself to go faster, ignoring the stabbing in his leg. When he reached the front door, he could hear the sharp, ragged gasps of Emma's breath. He sprinted inside as best he could with a crutch, his heart hammering in his throat. Would she be okay when he reached her? What if something had happened while he was gone?

Benjamin burst into the living room and tumbled onto the rag rug alongside the couch. His crutch clattered to the floor. "I'm here. I'm right beside you." He took Emma's hand. She squeezed and the strength of her grip startled him. He leaned forward and shifted his bad ankle so that he could stay there, huddled on the floor, as close to her as he could get.

"Don't leave me," Emma murmured. Sweat glistened on her face and he wiped it away. He tucked a strand of hair behind her ear that had fallen from her *kapp*. "I will never leave you," he said. And he meant it with all his heart.

Emma did not know her heart could be so full. Her perfect, tiny baby lay in her arms and she felt a love unlike any she had ever known before. She breathed in the scent of baby, closing her eyes as she inhaled.

"Are you ready to let people in now?" Elizabeth asked. Emma opened her eyes and reminded herself where she was. Everything had happened so quickly. By the time she reached Stoneybrook Farm, nothing had felt real anymore. The hours—or had it only been minutes?—had melted into a surreal blur of impossible pain followed by impossible joy. "They're eager to meet the *boppli* and make sure you're *oll recht*. Edna and Amos are here, and the Stoltzfus family, of course. But you don't have to see any of them until you're ready. It's up to you." Elizabeth made a notation on the chart in her hands, then capped the pen. She was Mennonite and wore a simple calf-length dress with a delicate floral print paired with sensible black shoes. A round, white head covering was pinned over her bun. The covering was small enough that most of her curly, brown hair was visible. She had been no-nonsense during the labor, but the spray of freckles across her nose and the sparkle in her eyes made her appear softer now.

Emma looked at the closed door. "I didn't mean to have the baby here. Whose room is this?"

"Miriam's. And don't worry about that. It's a good thing you came here when labor started so suddenly. Benjamin did everything right."

A warm glow spread through Emma, melting into the love she was already feeling for her baby. "*Ya*. He did."

"He's been crawling the walls out there." Elizabeth nodded toward the hallway. "I told him you're okay, but he won't believe it until he sees you." She gave a wry smile. "I don't see many fathers that excited about a new baby."

"He's not the father."

"I know. We talked about all that at your first appointment."

"Wait." Emma straightened up a little. "You mean..."

"Yes. That's exactly what I mean. He's more invested than a lot of the fathers I see." Elizabeth leaned forward and adjusted the quilt. "Now lie back down and rest. I'll let him in if you would like to see him now."

Emma let herself sink back into the pillows propped behind her head. But her heart was still beating a little too fast. "*Ya*. I want to see him."

Memories flooded through her. They came as snapshots that had survived the haze of pain, like the photographs that *Englischers* organize into albums. She couldn't quite remember all the details or the order of how it had all happened. What she did remember clearly was that Benjamin had scooped her up and carried her to safety. She remembered how warm his body had felt, how he had been strong and gentle at the same time. She remembered his heartbeat tapping in her ear. She had listened to it, held on to it as she rode out a wave of pain. She remembered how he had huddled next to her until Elizabeth came. He had held her hand and refused to let go, even after the midwife rushed into the living room.

Elizabeth opened the bedroom door and a low murmur of voices drifted into the room before the door shut again, leaving Emma in silence. There was only the soft, sweet sigh of her baby's breath. A moment later the door flew open and Benjamin rushed inside. He hobbled to her side using a crutch. She could see him wince in pain each time his left foot grazed the floor.

"You're hurt," she said.

"*Ach*, it's nothing. The midwife fixed it up after she took care of you. I'll be *gut* as new soon."

"But—"

"We'll talk about it later. Right now, I want to

know if you're *oll recht*. That's all that matters to me." He scanned her carefully, his face creased with concern. Then his eyes moved to the little bundle in her arms. "You and the *boppli*."

Emma patted the bed beside her. "Sit. You need to take the weight off that ankle."

Benjamin sank down onto the mattress. "You haven't told me if you're *oll recht*." His eyes were dark and serious.

"We're fine. Both of us. Everything's *oll recht*." Emma released a happy, exhausted sigh. "*Nee*, everything is *wunderbar*."

The crease in Benjamin's forehead relaxed and he grinned. "Can I hold the baby?" His smile faltered a little. "I'm sorry. I shouldn't have asked. It's not my... It's not my place to ask."

"Of course you can hold him."

"Him?"

"*Ya*. It's a boy."

"Elizabeth didn't tell us. She wanted you to get the chance."

"She didn't tell you the name either, did she?"

Benjamin slid his hands under the fragile, sleeping newborn and slowly lifted him. He glanced at Emma and she nodded. "You're doing fine. Just like that."

Benjamin drew the baby to his chest and held him there, marveling at his perfect, miniature features. "*Nee*, she didn't tell us the name. What is it?"

Emma's attention moved from the baby up to Benjamin's eyes. She swallowed hard and hoped that she had made the right decision. "Benjamin."

"*Ya?* What is it?"

Emma laughed and shook her head. "*Nee*, that's his name. Benjamin."

"Oh!" He gave her a look of surprise, then took the baby's hand in his. The newborn fingers looked so sweet and small in Benjamin's big, calloused hand. "You named him for me!" Emma had never seen him look so joyful.

"After the way you helped me..." Emma faltered and looked down. "I mean, if you hadn't been here..." She traced a quilt square with her finger. There was so much more she wanted to say, but she was too afraid to say it. Benjamin had rescued her in a way that made her believe that he might be in with love her. She had felt so connected to him during those terrifying minutes while they waited for the midwife together. It had not felt like friendship. It had felt like much, much more.

But still, she did not know. And now she felt the bright flush of shame creep up her cheeks. Maybe she had been too bold to believe that, to name her baby after him. Her mother always used to warn, *people believe what they want to believe*.

"Is that the only reason?" Benjamin asked. Something about the way he said it felt raw and real.

"*Nee,*" Emma said softly.

Seconds ticked by. The room was very, very quiet.

"Boys are named after their *daeds*."

Emma wasn't sure what he meant by that. She was afraid to ask.

"I hope I'm not overstepping my bounds, but this is my one shot to say this. If you don't like what I'm about to say, just tell me and I'll never bring it up again. You don't owe me anything. I hope you understand that."

Emma nodded. "I do. I can be myself with you. Always. No one else has ever made me feel that way."

He nodded slowly. "I'd like to be his *daed*, Emma. If that's what you would like. If that's what you meant by naming him Benjamin."

Emma's eyes shot up to his. "*Ya!* That is what I want."

"You're sure?"

"Benji, I've never been more certain of anything in my life." Emma watched him holding her son—*their* son—and she knew that this was everything she had ever wanted.

"Does this mean you'll marry me?" Benjamin's expression was still cautious, uncertain.

"Ya."

A wave of emotion passed over Benjamin's face. His arms tightened around the baby. "I've loved you for as long as I can remember, Emma."

"You..." Emma froze. Had she heard him right?

Benjamin hesitated. "You're everything to me." He flexed his jaw and looked away. "You've always been everything to me."

"But..." Emma shook her head. "I didn't know." She tried to think back, to organize the memories. Benjamin had always been there, loping along with that happy-go-lucky lopsided grin. He had loved her that entire time?

"I know that you haven't always loved me and—"

"I always loved you," Emma interrupted.

"As a friend."

"Vell, ya. But that matters. Friendship is the best foundation for a marriage."

"Ya, but it's only the foundation. There needs to be more in addition to that. Can you love me back the way I love you? I don't want you to marry me unless you truly want to. I don't want you to be stuck for the rest of your life in a marriage without romantic love. Friendship is *gut*, but you deserve more than that. I don't want you

to settle. I know that there will be other men who would jump at the chance to marry you—"

"Benjamin. Stop."

Benjamin let her cut him off. He cleared his throat.

"I'm not settling. I've fallen in love with you. When I first came back to Bluebird Hills, I only thought of you as a friend. But that changed. Fast." She felt herself blush. "I want to marry *you*, Benji. There's no one else for me. There never will be."

Benjamin looked at her with adoration in his eyes. "Emma Yoder is going to be my *fraa*," he murmured out loud, as if he couldn't quite believe it. "I'm going to make you happy. I promise."

"You always have, Benjamin." And she knew it was true. She knew the love had always been there, waiting to blossom, long before she ever realized it.

"And now, I always will," Benjamin said.

"We'll make each other happy." Emma reached out and touched their sleeping baby. "All of us, together."

Epilogue

The days passed in a blur of joy and excitement. Everything felt shiny and new. They went ahead with the wedding ceremony the following week. Everyone agreed it was best to make it official as soon as possible. Emma and Baby Benjamin moved to Stoneybrook Farm right after the service.

The day of the move, Emma hesitated when she reached the front door. Everything felt familiar and right—Ollie's low whine, Belinda honking in the distance, the soft chime of bells as the goats grazed nearby. But she was not sure that she was welcome.

Miriam opened the screen door, nodded, and ushered her in.

Emma clutched her baby tightly and gathered her courage to say what needed to be said. She felt strengthened by Benjamin's presence as he stood beside her, carrying her brown leather suitcase. "You didn't stop the wedding, but that doesn't mean you're *oll recht* with the marriage.

Am I going to be *willkumm* here?" Emma's heart pounded in her throat. Confrontation scared her, but not knowing the truth felt worse. She could not bear living the rest of her life in awkward, hurtful silence, suspecting that Benjamin's sisters disapproved of the match and wanted her gone.

Miriam let out a long exhale. "Oh, Emma. I owe you an apology."

"You what?"

Emma was not sure she had heard quite right. "*Kumme* in. We all need to talk."

The entire extended family gathered around the kitchen table. Amanda set out spice cake and hot black coffee, then nodded to Miriam.

"*Vell*, it isn't easy to say this, so I'll just go ahead and say it." Miriam looked up from her coffee cup. A muscle in her cheek jumped. Emma could tell she was stepping out of her comfort zone.

Benjamin leaned back in his chair, steepled his fingers, and smiled. He was enjoying this. Emma relaxed a little.

"I shouldn't have tried to keep you and Benjamin apart. I'm sorry."

"We all are," Amanda added.

"*Ya,*" Naomi said.

"I wish I had done more to support you," Leah said. "I hope you know I was on your side."

"I did," Emma said. "It meant a lot."

"I hope you can forgive us and we can start over," Miriam said. "I know it will take time…" She frowned. "I don't expect you to want to be friends right away. Not after the way we treated you."

"I would like to start over," Emma said. "But I need to know something first. What changed your mind? Or are you just saying this because you don't have a choice, now that I've married into the family?"

Miriam shook her head. *"Ach, nee."*

"You don't know Miriam if you think she'd just pretend that everything is *oll recht*," Amanda said. A round of nervous laughter passed around the table.

"She says what she thinks," Leah said.

"Whether we want her to or not," Benjamin added.

Another round of laughter.

"I saw that you love each other," Miriam said after the laughter died down. "And I saw that you balance each other."

"We were afraid you'd lead him into trouble," Amanda said. "You know, encourage him to jump the fence, or something."

"But then we realized that he needs you," Naomi said. "He's himself around you. He feels safe and supported. And, I think you feel the same way around him."

"I do," Emma said softly.

"So," Miriam said. "We should have recognized that from the beginning. We shouldn't have assumed the worst about you. I was afraid of losing Benjamin, afraid of a lot of things. And it blinded me to how *gut* you are for him. It blinded me to a lot of things. I'm sorry."

Emma let the words sink in. She knew it would take time for the hurt to mend in her heart, but she knew that it would mend because Benjamin's sisters meant what they said. They wanted to make things right. "I'm willing to start over," Emma said after a moment.

"Danki," Miriam said. She hesitated, then placed her hand on top of Emma's and squeezed. The gesture was awkward, but it felt right. Emma knew that it was the beginning of a true friendship. Miriam let go of Emma's hand and smiled. "You know when I really saw the truth?"

"When?"

"When you stopped working here. I knew you were sacrificing your happiness for what you thought was best for him. That's an act of true, unselfish love." Miriam looked down, into her cup of black coffee. "And I knew that I was the reason you felt like you had to give up any chance with him."

"I think I understand now. It wasn't really about me."

Miriam's eyes moved back up to Emma's. "That's right. It took me a long time to see that, though. And I hurt you both because I couldn't see that the problem was actually me, not you."

"We all make mistakes," Emma said. "We all make the wrong choice sometimes. But *Gott* turns that around, ain't so?" Emma smiled down at the baby in her arms. "He works it all out for *gut*."

The tension in Miriam's face loosened. Her eyes crinkled in a genuine smile. "We don't deserve you, Emma."

Emma felt free inside. She would not be judged here. She would be appreciated and loved. This was her home, now. Forever.

She no longer felt the shame that had once consumed her. Benjamin's love had helped her realize her worth. So did the support from his sisters. And, of course, the steadfast encouragement that Edna and Amos continued to give. Emma had finally realized that she deserved to be accepted. She deserved to be respected. She knew there would always be whispers about her, but those whispers had lost their power.

As Baby Benjamin grew, so did the goat milk soap business. Emma had been right to believe in Benjamin's vision. Soon, they were selling more than they could make. They had a bustling stand at the Bluebird Hills Farmers Market every Saturday. Benjamin put up a sign at the end of the Stoneybrook Farm driveway that read *Homemade Goat Milk Soap. Englisch* tourists veered off the highway and drove their cars up to the farmhouse to buy directly from the family. The Millers stocked Stoneybrook Farm Soap at Aunt Fannie's Amish Gift Shop. The scented bars made the entire aisle smell like lavender and lemon, so they flew off the shelves.

Emma loved seeing the satisfaction on Benjamin's face when they restocked the empty shelf. He had succeeded. No, they had succeeded, together. And that success went so much further than a business endeavor. They had clung to each other, despite the obstacles. They had proved their love to everyone.

But more importantly, they were happy. They were a family. Sometimes, in the cool of the evening, as winter crept closer and they sat on the porch after dinner, Emma could barely believe anyone could be that happy. As the sun set over the farmland and the distant sunflower field fell into shadow, Benjamin liked to hold her hand, their baby snuggled between them, the chain creaking on the porch swing.

"I love you," he whispered into her ear. "You and our *boppli*." His breath felt warm against her skin, contrasting the cold breeze that whispered through the yard and sent the fall leaves spiraling into the air.

"I love you too," Emma said as Baby Benjamin stirred in her arms.

They watched the stars appear, each one winking awake as the sky bruised purple and stillness fell across the pastureland. Emma felt a sense of amazement at how *Gott* had given her the happily-ever-after that she had not believed possible. She had found love where it had always been—with her best friend. The man who would always understand her, support her, and respect her. The man who had been meant for her all along.

* * * * *

Dear Reader,

It has been a joy spending time with you in Bluebird Hills. I have loved sharing stories about the colorful characters in this quaint little village. We have come to the end of the series and I can't think of a better way to close it out than with Benjamin's and Emma's story. I hope we can all learn to recognize our intrinsic, God-given worth, just as they did.

Even though the Bluebird Hills series is over, I have good news! You will still be able to visit this idyllic farming community in upcoming books. My next series will follow Miriam, Amanda, Naomi, and Leah as they find love. Your favorite characters will return alongside new ones. And, of course, there will be plenty of adorable goats as well as my favorite animal in the series, Belinda the guard goose.

Be on the lookout for my next novel so you can meet me at Stoneybrook Farm to discover which sister will be tumbling headfirst into an unexpected romance.

Love always,
Virginia Wise